FIGHT FOR THE LAZY M

A Western

R. Annan

Fight for the Lazy M
Copyright 2014 by R. Annan
WGA Reg. #: R31247

Edition 1.2

One Vision Publishing
Print Book ISBN: 978-1-942338-10-9
E-Book ISBN: 978-1-942338-11-6

Western books by R. Annan:

Fight for The Lazy M
The Gunfighter in Winter
Long Ride to Hell's Kitchen
Owl Hawks
Gunfight at Barfield Springs
Shootout at Sanctuary City
Last Days of a Gunfighter
The Red Bandana

Coming Soon: Clay Jared Westerns

Dedication

To

Sergeant Major Anthony R. Annan, US Army (Ret.)

1.

It was about an hour before sundown, in July of 1881, when Rice Farrell, Curley Barnes, and Tardy Whipple rode across the double line of railroad tracks into the cattle depot at Brent's Ford, Kansas. They went slowly down the main street. People stared at them and recognized them for the professional gunslingers that they were, and the street very quickly became empty.

One man, Cleet Dagston, stood in the shadows on the porch of his real estate office. He watched them with keen interest as they passed by. Dagston was the prime driving force in Brent's Ford. He owned every business in town except Nesbit's Barber Shop, Price's Mercantile Store, Goodman's Stable, and Flower's Dance Hall. The town, for all practical purposes, was Cleet Dagston's, and he kept a close eye on it.

Farrell and his men stopped in front of the C-D Saloon, adjacent Dagston's office. They tied their mounts to the hitching rail next to three other horses, went up the steps, and stood on the porch looking around.

"Looks like a one-horse town, boys," Farrell said.

Curley Barnes chuckled. "It looks like the pimple on a dog's rump, if you ask me."

"You think they's got some purty girls around here?" Tardy Whipple asked.

"We won't be here long enough to find out," Farrell said. "We're gonna wet our whistles and keep going. I wanna be in Cheneyville by morning so we can hit the bank and head out for the Devil's Den."

"Did you notice the name on most of the businesses, and the bank? It looks like somebody name of Dagston owns just about everything in sight," Barnes said.

Farrell nodded. "Yeah, I noticed that, too. Especially the bank."

The trio went into the saloon and stood for a moment looking the place up and down. It was poorly lit with several overhanging oil lamps. The only customers were three cowhands playing cards at a table in the back. They were having a good time among themselves, drinking, joking, and kidding around.

To Farrell's right, a big bear of a bartender stood behind the bar smoking a cigar and cleaning drinking glasses.

"My name is Charley," the bartender said. "What kin I do ya for?"

"Three rot-guts, Charley," Farrell said.

"Passing through?" Charley asked while he set up the shot glasses and poured the whiskey.

"Yeah," Farrell said.

Curley Barnes asked, "What kind of town is this? It don't look like much."

"It's a cattle shipping depot. Brent's Ford."

"Any girls around here?" Tardy Whipple asked.

Charley chuckled. "There's a dance hall down the street, if you're looking for women."

"I saw your jailhouse as we came in," Farrell said. "It looks more like an outhouse."

"Some days it smells like one, too," Charley said.

"Is it always this quiet?"

"It gets livelier on Friday nights and weekends."

Curley Barnes chuckled. "That's a cow town for you."

"Got a Marshal?" Farrell asked casually.

"The one we have was hired by Mr. Dagston. Dumbest Marshal I ever seen!" Charley followed that with a chuckle.

Farrell smiled. "That's how I like them. This Dagston, looks like this is his town."

"You might say that."

Charley poured another round. Farrell laid a coin down.

"Heck, boss, let's go on to Cheneyville," Tardy Whipple said.

"Relax," Farrell said. "Have another belt." He nodded towards the back table. "Who's playing cards?"

"Some cow pokes from the Lazy M spread."

Farrell pulled a gold double-eagle from his pocket and laid it on the bar. "Give us a bottle, friend. Keep the change."

Farrell took the bottle from Charley. He motioned to his two pals. They grabbed their shot glasses and followed their chief to the back of the saloon where the game was going on.

"Open game?" Farrell asked.

Earl, the loudest of the three Lazy M hands, looked up. When he saw the bottle in Farrell's hand, he smiled.

"Sure is, mister," Earl said. His voice was thick from drink. Farrell pulled up a chair and sat down. Curley and Tardy sat off to one side to watch.

"My name is Farrell."

"I'm Ben. This is Frank. The loud one is Earl," the youngest Lazy M hand said.

Unnoticed by the card players, the bat-wing doors opened quietly. Cleet Dagston stepped silently up to the bar, motioning to Charley not to speak. Dagston went over to one side, in the shadows, and watched the card players.

After only two hands, the Lazy M cowhand named Earl started on a winning streak. He took three hands in a row, lost one, took four, then lost two and took five more. From then on he took almost every pot.

"I'm sure hot tonight!" Earl bragged.

"Yeah, too hot, cowboy," Farrell said.

Earl froze and glared at Farrell. "What was that, mister?"

Ben put a hand on Earl's arm. "It's getting late, Earl, maybe we should be getting back to the Lazy M."

"He's not going any place," Farrell said coldly.

Earl quickly got up, overturning his chair with a bang.

"You sayin' I'm cheatin' mister?"

"Sit down, kid," Farrell said.

"Come on!" Frank urged his friend. "Cool down Earl!"

"We don't want no trouble, mister," Ben said.

Earl took a threatening stance, with his right arm out, his hand by his gun. "Go ahead and say it, mister!" His hand moved closer to his holster. "Come on, I dare you, say what yer a thinkin'!"

"Whose deck is this?" Farrell asked Ben.

"It's Earl's," Ben said.

"It's most likely marked with..."

Farrell never got to finish. The Lazy M man went for his gun. Farrell's own hands moved with lightning speed. A single shot rang out, echoing about the room. Earl was dead before he hit the floor.

Everyone else froze in place, speechless, staring down at Earl's body. Farrell holstered his gun.

"Take the pot and take him home and bury him boys." Farrell said as he closely inspected the cards. He shrugged. "Maybe I was wrong."

Suddenly the town Marshal came rushing in through the bat-wing doors He stopped to stare questioningly at Charley. The bartender pointed to the men in the back. The Marshal looked confused for a moment. Finally he cleared his throat, nodded, and went to the back table. Looking down, he saw the body. He flinched.

"Who did it?" Marshal Leach asked.

"I did, Marshal," Farrell said

Dagston came out of the shadows and up to them. The Marshal nodded and sort of saluted.

"Mr. Dagston, sir."

"Good evening, Marshal Leach."

"I was just on my rounds when I heard the shot."

"It was self-defense. I saw the whole thing," Dagston said.

"Self-defense, are you sure about that, sir?"

"Ask Frank and Ben. They'll tell you."

"Yeah, Marshal," Ben said grudgingly, "it was."

"I'll help you with the paperwork, Marshal. And so will mister, ah..." Dagston looked at Farrell.

"Farrell, Rice Farrell. I'd be glad to answer any questions, Marshal."

Marshal Leach studied Farrell's face a moment, then nodded and turned to Ben and Frank. "Go on, boys, take Earl back to the Lazy M. Tell the Gavins I'll soon be out to see them."

Ben scooped up the money and shoved it in his shirt pockets. He and Frank picked Earl up. They took him outside. In a few minutes they rode away.

"Come over to the jailhouse and make out a statement," the lawman told Farrell.

"Sure, Marshal."

"I'll go and make mine out too, Marshal," Dagston said.

An hour later, Dagston, Farrell, Barnes, and Whipple were sitting in Dagston's real estate office smiling and drinking whiskey.

"Thanks for the help, Dagston," Farrell said.

"You boys looking for a temporary, high paying job? Not permanent, mind you. Just until the job is done."

"Maybe, that depends," Rice Farrell said. "Right, boys?" Barnes and Whipple nodded.

Dagston pointed to a map on the wall. It showed Brent's Ford. The railroad passed through it, made a big loop around a mountain range, and back down to the town of Cheneyville. Cheneyville was directly opposite Brent's Ford but with a fifty or so mile distance between them.

Dagston took a yardstick and pencil off his desk. He drew a straight line from Brent's Ford to Cheneyville.

"You know what I just did, Mr. Farrell?"

Farrell nodded. "You just saved the railroad a good hundred miles around that mountain range."

Dagston chuckled. "Very astute of you, sir! Very astute."

"So," Farrell said, "What's the problem?"

"The problem is the Lazy M ranch. It stands dead center between Cheneyville and Brent's Ford. The Gavins own it and refuse to sell," Dagston said. "The rest of the land around the Lazy M is government land. The railroad can lease that with no problem."

"How do we fit in?" Farrell asked.

"Fix it so Gavin must sell the Lazy M. It's as simple as that," Dagston said.

"How?"

"Hurt the Lazy M, just like you did tonight. But hurt it more, and don't tell me about it. Just do what you have to do to make him sell."

"Kill a few more of their cowhands? Is that what you want?"

Dagston thought a moment. "Ah, no, not if you can get around it. Put a good scare into them. Make it so nobody will hire on at the Lazy M. After tonight that should be easy."

"What about the Marshal?"

"Don't worry about him."

Farrell looked over at Curley and Tardy. They nodded. "We don't come cheap for this kind of work," he said.

Dagston wrote an amount on a piece of paper. He shoved it at Farrell. Farrell whistled. "Boys, I think we just found some easy pickings. Cheneyville can wait." He shook hands with Dagston, and then said, "This Gavin, does he have a family?"

"A wife and a girl, seventeen. A boy, fifteen, and another sixteen."

"What's the girl look like?" Farrell asked.

"Pretty as a picture and well grown, too if you know what I mean," Dagston said. "Why?"

"Nothin' just curious. Yeah, we'll take the job."

"You're on, then?" Dagston asked, just to make sure.

"Yeah," Farrell said, "we're on."

Dagston poured another round. He held up his glass for a toast. "To the end of the Lazy M."

Out on the road west, heading for the Lazy M, young Ben, and Frank rode slowly along in the pale-white moonlight. A coyote howled in the hills north of Brent's

Ford. Its mournful voice cut the night like a knife. Young Ben stared ahead at the road that looked like a long silver ribbon that led back to the Lazy M.

2.

Jim Gavin and his family had just made a purchase at Price's Mercantile and he was guiding his one-horse buckboard up the main street of Brent's Ford, heading west, out of town. His wife Mary sat beside him. His daughter Sarah and his two sons, Ray the youngest and Ed the oldest, were sprawled in the back with the newly purchased supplies and food.

Dagston, Farrell, Curley, and Tardy stood on the porch of Dagston's Real Estate Office, looking down the road, watching as the Gavin's wagon got closer. At a certain point, Dagston and Farrell stepped out to intercept them. Gavin pulled the horse to a stop. Farrell moved in close and took hold of the horse's halter, stroking the animal's neck and whispering to it.

"What do you want, Dagston?" Jim Gavin asked.

"I'll give you twenty dollars an acre, Gavin," Dagston said. "That's as high as I can go. You'd be a fool to turn it down."

Gavin glanced at his wife. She shook her head, no.

"We're not interested in selling just yet, Mr. Dagston," Gavin said. He stared at Rice Farrell. "Would you mind telling your man to let go of my horse?"

Farrell walked slowly around the horse. He stopped next to Mary Gavin, staring at her. She stared back, fascinated for a moment, as the gunslinger saluted her.

"Rice Farrell, ma'am," Farrell said smoothly.

"We have a saying in Brent's Ford, Mr. Farrell," Mary Gavin said. She smiled politely.

"Oh? And what's that, Mrs. Gavin?"

"Both clergymen and gunmen wear black, but gunmen don't carry a Bible."

Farrell chuckled. "How true, ma'am, how true."

The two young boys leaned over the side of the buckboard and stared wide-eyed at Farrell.

"You're a gunslinger, ain't you, mister?" Ray said. Ed poked his younger brother to shut him up.

"That's not nice, son," Mary Gavin said, looking back at Ray.

Farrell walked slowly up to the children, letting them have a good look at his gunman's attire, his black hat, black shirt, black Levis, and black, oiled, leather boots. His buckskin vest was adorned with silver Mexican conchas. Young Ray was hypnotized.

"You must be Ray," Farrell said, "and you're Ed." He looked at Sarah and smiled warmly. "And you must be Sarah. And mighty big and pretty for seventeen."

"How'd you know my name, mister?" Sarah said with a sneer.

"Call me Rice, Miss Sarah," Farrell said smoothly. "You sure are pretty, Miss Sarah. You ever been to a dance?"

"That's none of your business, mister!"

"I'd sure like to dance with you, Miss Sarah, I sure would. You're so pretty."

Suddenly Jim Gavin leered at Dagston. He nervously cleared his throat.

"Mr. Dagston, I don't like the way your man is talking to my little girl. It's downright disrespectful!"

"He's right there, Gavin," Dagston said. "Go ahead and tell him."

Jim Gavin suddenly realized two things. He, himself, was wearing a gun and now he was about to face a professional gunman, a man who made his living by the gun. Secondly, he knew, after what had happened to his cowhand, Earl, he could never beat Rice Farrell to the draw. No, not, after what had happened to Earl.

His mind was racing, thinking how to get out of this dilemma alive, when Mary Gavin put a hand on his arm.

"Let's go home, Jim!" she said urgently.

Gavin snapped the reins and yelled at the horse. It jerked forward. The children held on as the buckboard raced away down the road and out of town.

Farrell looked after them, chuckling. "So that's Jim Gavin, huh?"

"Yes, and he still won't sell!" Dagston muttered angrily.

Just then Marshal Leach came from an alleyway. He approached Dagston.

"Looks like the Gavins left in a hurry," he said. "Is anything wrong?"

Dagston chuckled. "No, Marshal, his wife suddenly remembered she left the stew pot boiling."

The Marshal nodded. He smiled as he walked away.

Farrell casually rolled a cigarette. He lit it, and blew smoke in the air. He followed Dagston back to the CD porch.

"Is that lawman as dumb as he acts?" Farrell asked.

"He's dumber!" Dagston said.

"He keeps staring at me," Farrell said. "That irritates the hell out of me."

"It's just his way," Dagston said. "He thinks he's a real Marshal." They all laughed. Finally Dagston said, "So, now that you've seen Gavin, what do you think, Farrell?"

Farrell stared at the cigarette between his fingers, and gave the question some thought.

"I'd don't like his face. I'm for making her a widow," he said coldly. There was no emotion in his voice.

"What, you mean kill him?" Dagston said, startled.

"Why not? It's faster that way," Farrell said. "Besides, if you scare off a few of his cowboys, he'll hire more. Maybe even get a few gun hands. There are hundreds looking for work these days. But with Gavin gone, she'll most likely decide to sell."

"But, last night all we talked about was scaring off a few of his hired hands!"

"That was before I saw his face. He's a yellow belly. He was so scared I could smell it."

"But I never mentioned killing him!"

"This has nothing to do with you. It's between me and him. I don't like his yellow belly face."

"It's too risky, Farrell. People will know."

"Not the way I'm gonna do it they won't."

"I'm not so sure about that."

"Look, it's the fastest and surest way to get that spread, unless you're ready to wait until Gavin dies of old age." Farrell paused to let his words sink in. "You want that ranch, or don't you, Dagston?"

Cleet Dagston agonized for a moment, thinking. The situation was quickly getting out of hand. He didn't like losing control of things. Maybe there was some other way. But, that didn't seem likely. He had been patient with Jim Gavin for a long, long time. He made Gavin several good offers but Gavin had stubbornly refused to budge.

Dagston finally sighed and nodded to Farrell. "It's your choice, not mine. Just keep me out of it."

"Okay, sure," Farrell said. Then, after a pause. "I've got another gun coming in. A friend of Tardy's is joining up with us."

"Alright, do what you want. As far as I'm concerned, we never spoke about this. Just get it done, then ride on. But don't get me involved, you hear?"

Farrell nodded, thinking, *Oh, but you are involved, Dagston and Rice Farrell moves on when he's good and ready to move on and he ain't ready yet.*

3.

A week later, Rice Farrell, Curley Barnes, Tardy Whipple, and their new gunman Reb Smears, stood on the porch of the C-D Saloon. They were watching, with interest, the comings, and goings on Brent's Ford's main street. After a while, they took note of a young, dust-covered cowboy with red hair walking his horse slowly past them. He wore a wide brimmed hat with Mexican conchas along the brim. It was pulled down low, casting a shadow over his face.

Curley said, "That kid's a Texan."

Reb Smears asked, "How do you know?"

"Because, I'm from Texas. That kid's got Texas written all over him."

Reb chuckled. "He looks like a poor, dumb-assed cow poke to me, Texas or no Texas!"

Suddenly Tardy Whipple perked up. He pointed up the road. "Looky there! What's that a coming?" The red headed rider was quickly forgotten.

"Looks like the Gavin woman," Curley said.

Cleet Dagston, walking up from his office, had also seen Mary Gavin's buckboard. He joined the others in watching. Sarah Gavin sat alongside her mother while young Ray Gavin sat on a pile of burlap sacks in the back. As they came alongside the C-D Saloon Dagston waved, but Mary Gavin ignored him and kept on going.

"She's got your number, Dagston," Farrell chuckled.

"The stuck-up bitch! Somebody should tell her what her husband is up to with that sweet thing at the dance hall."

Reb Smears stepped down into the street.

"Where you going, Smears?" Farrell asked.

"That young one, she sure is pretty," Smears said. "I gotta get a closer look at that sweet thing."

"I'd be careful if I were you," Curley said.

"I'm a lady's man from way back!" Smears bragged.

Farrell cut in. "He means the mother. She'll chop you down without so much as blinking."

"Hell, I kin handle momma, alright!"

21

"I wouldn't go bothering them, if I was you," Curley said.

"You ain't me, Curley," Smears boasted. "I'm irresistible to all women." He went down the road in the direction of the buckboard.

Dagston cleared his throat. "Get rid of that one, Farrell," he said.

"How come?"

"He don't listen. I want him gone today," Dagston insisted.

"He's damn fast with a gun," Farrell said. "We're going to need him."

"He ain't got no sense, he's stupid. Fire him!"

Farrell shrugged. "Okay, but it'll cost fifty-bucks." Dagston nodded. He gave Farrell the money.

Down the road, the redheaded Texan disappeared into Price's Mercantile just as Mary Gavin pulled up with her buckboard. Young Ray jumped down and ran around to take the reins and tie it to the rail.

Reb Smears walked boldly up to Sarah Gavin and smiled. "Come on, little darling, let old Reb help you!" He offered his hand to her.

Mary Gavin glanced over. "Ignore him, Sarah, he's a Dagston man."

"Get away from my sister, you polecat!" Little Ray yelled.

Smears held his palms out and backed away, chuckling. "Okay, sonny boy! Okay!"

The Gavins went into Price's Mercantile. Smears waited a moment then slowly followed them in.

The inside of Dell Price's Mercantile was lit by the afternoon sun coming through its many windows. There were racks of clothing and stacks of goods all around. There was something for everybody, from candy to bullets, nails to dresses, tools to cough medicine, and other sundries. For male or female, Dell Price had it all.

The redheaded cowboy was at the counter, just about to ask for a box of shells, when the Gavins came in. When his eyes fell upon Sarah Gavin, he thought he had died and gone to heaven. Right then he decided he needed to spend some more time browsing around the store.

Mary Gavin came up to the counter and handed Dell Price a list of things she needed. The cowboy, ignoring her, kept his eyes on young Sarah as she and her little brother went down a clothing isle, out of sight.

A second later, Reb Smears came quietly in. He stopped and looked around for Sarah Gavin. Upon hearing her voice, he walked in its general direction. He soon found her by a rack of dresses and came up close. The girl ignored him.

Suddenly Smears reached a hand out and touched Sarah Gavin's golden-blond hair. She spun around and slapped him as hard as she could, sending him back on his heels. He felt his jaw and blinked in surprise.

"Damn, that felt good!" Smears chuckled. "But you owe me a kiss for that one!"

"I'd rather kiss a snake, you fool!"

"Give it a try, girl," Smears said. "Maybe you'll like it."

Just as he made a grab for her, he felt a sharp pain in his groin area. Before he realized it, he was down on his knees, gasping for air, as the girl and her brother disappeared.

Suddenly Smears was aware that someone close by was chuckling. He glanced up and saw the redheaded cowboy.

"What the hell you gawking about, fellah?"

"Say a prayer for me while you're down there, slick."

Reb Smears got to his feet. He glared at the redhead. "How'd you like to get your teeth smashed in?"

"No, sir? I wouldn't like that, at all."

"Then you'd best move on, cowboy, or I'll tighten your cinch!" The redhead held up his hands in peace, backed away, and went behind another rack, out of sight.

Reb Smears glanced around for Sarah. He saw she was gone and went off to find her. In a few moments he saw her with her mother, at the counter. He came up close to her, staring at her, smiling. Sarah pushed him away. Her mother glared at Smears.

"I'm warning you, fellah, leave us be!" she growled.

"I'm just trying to be friendly, ma'am," Smears said.

Little Ray Gavin got between Smears and his sister. "You better vamoose, you varmint!" he shouted.

25

"Oooooooh! I'm real scared, sonny. I'm shaking in my boots!"

The redhead came out from an aisle. As he walked past he nodded to the Gavins then shoulder-butted Smears up against the counter, knocking the wind out of him.

"Ooops! Sorry." The redhead said He turned his back on Smears and walked slowly toward the door.

"Stop, you son-of-a-bitch! Draw!" Smears growled.

The kid raised his hands high and turned around to face Smears. He nodded. "Not here," he said, "let's go outside."

Smears rushed up to the redhead and waved the barrel of his Colt under his nose. "Let's go, you stupid clod-hopper! I'm gonna blow your face off!" He rushed past him and out into the street.

The redhead walked calmly back to the counter. He put a coin down and took a stick of root beer flavored candy from a candy jar. He handed it to Sarah Gavin.

"Would you hold this for me, ma'am?"

Sarah Gavin took the piece of candy. She was about to say something but before she could say a word, the redhead had gone through the door.

"He's going to be killed, momma," Sarah said sadly.

Mary Gavin turned to Dell Price. "Can't you stop them, Dell? Maybe get the Marshal?" Dell Price only shrugged. He shook his head. There was nothing he could do.

4.

From their position on the porch of the C-D Saloon, Dagston, Farrell, Curley, and Tardy saw their new man, Reb Smears rush out of Price's Mercantile into the street, waving his gun and shouting profanities.

"Oh, no!" Farrell groaned. "What the hell is he up to now?"

"We'd best go down and see what's going on," Dagston said with a big, disgusted sigh.

By the time they got close to the mercantile, the redhead was slowly and calmly getting into position. He had his hands up as he backed away, facing Smears who was pointing his gun at him.

"Come on, you dumb ass!" Smears screamed. "Hurry up and get set! I'm gonna shoot both yer ears off!"

People nearby began to run for cover. Mary, Ray, Sarah, and Mr. Price stood in the doorway of the mercantile, staring with concerned looks on their faces.

Dagston, Farrell, Barnes, and Tardy Ripple stood in the entrance of a nearby alleyway, watching.

"It's that Texan," Curley Barnes said. "Smears is bracing him."

"Yeah," Farrell chuckled. "The redhead can kiss his ass adios! Smears is one of the fastest draws in the territory."

"Yeah?" Curley said. "Well, look how far away the Texan is. He ain't nobody's fool."

The redhead stopped a good distance away from Smears, his hands still held high to indicate he wasn't ready yet.

"Come on, you fence mender! Draw! Let's see what you got! Slap leather!"

"I think you got the jump on me, fellah, with your gun already out!" he yelled back at Smears.

Smears jammed his Colt back in its holster. "I'm counting to three and then I'm gonna kill ya!"

"Can you count that high?" the redhead chuckled.

"You're dead, you sidewinder!"

Without warning, Smears drew his Colt with lightning speed and rushed forward, to close the gap, firing a shot as

29

he went. Suddenly he stopped. His legs turned to rubber. He swayed drunkenly from side to side and dropped his gun in the dirt. There was a surprised look on his face as he stared blankly at the redheaded kid who stood there slowly putting another bullet in his Colt to replace the one he had just put in Smear's heart.

Smear's knees buckled and he hit the dirt face first.

Suddenly the Marshal came bursting through the group of on lookers. Dagston also broke through the crowd. He stared down at Smear's body and muttered low, so no one could hear, "You're fired!"

Marshal Leach walked up to the redhead. "I'll take your gun, kid."

Dagston looked up. "Now, hold on a minute, Marshal. I saw the whole thing. This young man had no choice but to defend himself."

"I'm Sorry, Mr. Dagston, but he's gotta stand trial. It's the law."

"Fine, Marshal, a trial it is," Dagston said. He looked into the crowd of witnesses. "What's the verdict, folks? Self-defense or not? Tell the Marshal your verdict here and now!"

"Self-defense!" the crowd yelled.

"Look, Marshal," Dagston said, "why waste the citizens' money and time? Show some common sense, okay?"

"Who's gonna pay to bury the body?" the Marshal asked.

"How much?"

"A double- eagle," the Marshal said.

Dagston dug into his pocket and handed the Marshal two gold double-eagles. "Put some flowers on the grave."

The Marshal nodded and pointed a finger at two men he knew in the crowd. "Take him over to the undertaker, boys." The crowd lost interest and wondered off.

Rice Farrell stared at the redhead. "You want to try that with me, kid?'

"No, sir, not if I don't have to."

Farrell chuckled. "You ain't as dumb as you look, kid." He patted the redhead on the back.

"What's your name? Where you from?" Dagston asked.

"Art Haney. Kansas State Prison."

"Ex-con, are you?"

"No, sir. I was just visiting my uncle, Fred Smith. I'm from down around the Pecos River. Some people call me, Pecos Red."

Farrell's face lit up. "Sidewinder Smith, the train robber, is you uncle?"

"Yup! He's my uncle alright. You heard of him?"

"Christ! He's a legend, the old bastard!" Farrell chuckled.

"I've read stories about him in the pulp magazines," Dagston said. "Quite a man. Robbed from the rich and gave to the poor. The Robin Hood of train robbers."

"He's getting out on parole, soon," Haney said.

"I'd really like to meet him," Dagston said.

The Marshal stared closely at Haney. "So, what's your line of work, kid?"

"I'm legal, Marshal," Haney said.

"You looking for work?"

Haney shrugged and looked over at Sarah Gavin and smiled. "Maybe."

"Well, I could use a…"

"Hold it, Marshal," Dagston said. "The nephew of Sidewinder Smith is going to work for me!"

Mary Gavin stepped down from the porch. "He's working for me, Dagston. He doesn't want the type of dirty work you have in mind."

The Marshal looked at Art Haney. "Well, Pecos Red, from the Pecos River. What's it gonna be, son, working for me as deputy, or Mr. Dagston, or Mrs. Gavin?"

Art Haney shrugged uncertainly. "I'm not sure, Marshal? What would you do?"

"I don't know about you, son, but I'm partial to homemade apple pie. Are you partial to homemade apple pie?"

"I sure am," Haney chuckled. "I sure am."

"Then I'd go to work for Mrs. Gavin, out at the Lazy M. She makes the best apple pie this side of the Missouri Brakes," the Marshal said.

He didn't see the hateful look that Cleet Dagston gave him.

An hour later, with their purchases completed, Mary Gavin headed out of Brent's Ford with Art Haney riding by her side. Young Ray Gavin was busy in the back of the buckboard chewing on a stick of root beer candy and watching the town disappear in the distance.

It was afternoon when they rode through the gate, into the yard of the Lazy M, and up to the main house. Haney saw the barn and corral behind it, off to the right. The small bunkhouse was about twenty yards to the right of that. Behind the bunkhouse was a densely wooded hill looking down on the ranch. The rest of the land was rolling hills and open spaces. Haney could see cattle grazing in the distance.

Jim and Ed Gavin came out to meet them. Mary's husband stared at Haney.

"This is Earl's replacement, Art Haney," Mary said as she and the children got down.

It was then that Haney became conscious that Mary Gavin was wearing a man's shirt, trousers, boots, and hat. He hadn't noticed that before because his eyes were on Sarah.

"Jim Gavin," Gavin said, introducing himself, as Haney got down to shake his hand. He then turned to his wife. "Ah, did you discuss pay with Mr. Haney?"

"Don't worry about that," Haney cut in. "You can pay me in apple pies, if you want to." They all laughed. Haney and Sarah kept staring at each other.

Jim Gavin noticed that and said, "Ah, we do have one rule, though, Mr. Haney. The hired hands eat down in the bunkhouse. If you need anything special, why see me and I'll see what I can do."

Haney knew what Jim Gavin really meant was "Stay away from my daughter!"

"Yes, sir," Art Haney said.

"I'll take you down to meet the other fellows at the bunkhouse, Haney," Gavin said. The kid fell in behind his new boss. His horse whinnied and trotted up behind him, nudging Haney with his nose.

"Could I settle my horse down first, sir?"

"Of course," Gavin said. "We're not a big spread, son. I only have eight hands. Right now six of them are out pulling in some cattle that we'll take into town this week. At least Dagston doesn't own the stockyard and railroad."

After they fed and watered Haney's horse and bedded him down in the stable in the barn, they went over into the

35

bunkhouse where Ben and Frank were playing cards at the table in the middle of the room. All the windows were open and the bright sunlight lit up the one room structure. In one corner was a small, iron stove. The wash basin and stand were outside, by the door.

"Boys, this is Art Haney, come to work for us."

Ben put down his cards and stood up. He came close to Haney and stared at him. Suddenly he smiled and let out with a loud rebel yell.

"My God! If it ain't Pecos Red then my name ain't Ben Turner!" He turned to Jim Gavin. "Mr. Gavin, this kid is one of the fastest draws this side of the Pecos River!"

"Then you two must have a lot to talk about," Jim Gavin said, and left. He didn't seem to be much interested in the new man at all.

Haney, Frank, and Ben sat and talked over coffee. It wasn't long before the conversation turned to how Rice Farrell had gunned down Earl, in the CD Saloon.

"That Farrell, I never saw a man draw as fast as he him," Ben said. "Right, Frank?"

36

But Art Haney's mind was somewhere else. It was on the prettiest face this side of heaven.

5.

It was well after midnight when Jim Gavin left Flower's Dance Hall by the side stairs. A few hours earlier he had been at the cattlemen's meeting down at the stockyard building. After that he went straight up to Nelly Tulley's room. Four hours later, half drunk and exhausted, he was riding slowly along Brent's Ford's main street, heading back to the Lazy M, feeling guilty and swearing to himself he'd never cheat on his wife again. It was an empty vow that he had made many times before but knew he would never keep.

As he passed by, he never noticed the four figures standing in the darkness on the porch of Dagston's real estate office.

"Just like I said," Dagston muttered. "The end of every month, after the cattlemen's meeting. Him and Nelly Tulley."

"Yep, you were right, Dagston," Farrell said in a low voice. "And there won't be a better time than right now to put him away."

"Maybe you should just make it so he can't run the ranch for a while," Dagston said. "Cripple him up a little."

"What good will that do? She'll just get one of the cowhands to take over and ramrod the place."

"If she does, then we could hit them harder," Dagston said. He sounded nervous, unsure of himself. After a long silence, "Hell, you don't have to kill the man."

Farrell sneered. "What I do to him is up to me, Dagston. It's not your worry."

"Just bust him up bad enough so he'll never ride again that should do it!"

Farrell sneered. "You think so?"

"Yeah, sure."

Farrell chuckled and stepped off the porch, onto the street. "Yeah, sure. Come on boys, let's take a ride."

Curley Barnes and Tardy Whipple nodded. The three of them mounted their horses and moved out at a slow canter, heading out of town, in the direction of the Lazy M.

When Brent's Ford was behind them, they pulled their bandanas up over their noses, below their eyes, and pulled their hats down lower on their foreheads.

A sliver of pale moon laid a carpet of faint light on the road. Somewhere a coyote bayed mournfully.

"You hear that?" Tardy Whipple asked. "They say when they howl like that it means someone is gonna die."

Curley Barnes chuckled. "Sure, like they know ahead of time. Haw!"

They rode faster, and soon saw Jim Gavin. His mount was moving at a slow gait and he was slumped over, almost asleep in the saddle. When he heard them he suddenly became alert and stiffened. He turned his horse and stared back. The three mounted men came on with their heads down and went past him without a word. A few yards beyond they stopped, then turned, and spread out across the road.

Gavin looked at them for a moment. "I'm Jim Gavin. Let me pass." They didn't answer so he said, "What's going on, here?"

"You'll soon find out, mister," Farrell said.

Gavin squinted in the darkness. "Say, don't I know you? Your voice sounds familiar. You're that gunslinger Dagston hired!"

"You shouldn't have said that, Gavin."

"Why?"

"Because now I'll have to kill you!"

Gavin saw a flash of light but never saw the bullet coming. It killed him before the muzzle blast reached his ears. His body flipped backwards off his horse, and the horse sprinted away into the nearby woods.

"For crying out loud, Rice!" Tardy yelled. "You shot him!"

"I had to," Farrell said as he reloaded his gun. "He recognized me." Farrell got down and walked over to the body. He nudged it with his boot.

"Dagston ain't gonna like this," Curley Barnes said.

"It doesn't matter if he does or not," Farrell replied. "He's in as deep as we are."

Rice Farrell knelt down and searched Gavin's body, taking everything he could find out of his pants and shirt pockets.

"What are you doing that for?" Tardy asked.

"Somebody followed Gavin from the dance hall, then shot and robbed him," Farrell said. When he was finished, he got back on his horse. They were just about to leave when Farrell made a decision.

"You two go over there and put a slug in him," Farrell said.

"How come?" Tardy asked. "He's already dead, ain't he?"

"Just do like I said," Farrell insisted.

Curley and Tardy dismounted and walked over to the body and stood there staring down, a bit confused.

"Do it!" Farrell growled. He drew his gun "Or I'll put one in the both of you!"

The two took out their guns and shot Gavin in the chest, then came back to their horses and saddled up.

"Now we're all in it," Farrell said as he put his gun back in its holster. "If I hang, you both hang with me."

"Christ," Barnes said. "Now it's just her and the three kids. I don't like this, Rice."

"If it sticks in your craw, then you'd better ride on Curley," Farrell said. "But if I ever see you again, I'll have to kill you. So, think about that."

"You're really after the girl, ain't you, Rice?" Curley said.

Farrell nodded. "It'll be easier, now with Gavin out of the way."

"Whatta we gonna do with the body?" Tardy asked.

"Nothing. Somebody will find it in the morning," Farrell said.

"What if the coyotes find it first?" Curley asked.

Farrell shrugged. "You worry too much, Curley." He rode back towards Brent's Ford. Tardy and Curley fell in alongside him.

6.

Dagston was in his office behind his desk going over some paperwork by the light of an oil lamp when Rice Farrell, Curley, and Tardy came in. The two sidekicks sat down on the couch as their boss sat on the edge of Dagston's desk.

"How did it go?" Dagston asked, looking up.

"He's out of your way now, Dagston," Farrell said casually.

"You busted him up some, did you?"

"Oh, yeah! I busted him up, alright. You don't have to worry about yellow belly anymore." Farrell laughed.

Dagston froze. A flicker of fear crossed his eyes. He stared hard at Farrell.

"That wasn't what we had planned. You were only supposed to…"

"I know, but he recognized me." Dagston looked confused. Farrell went on, "It's best like this. We made it

44

look like somebody robbed him. There's no connection to me or you."

Dagston looked worried. "I'm in the clear, then?"

"Yep. You're in the clear."

Dagston sighed and relaxed. "Good."

"The Lazy M will be yours by next week."

Dagston let Farrell's words sink in for a moment. "You think so?"

"Sure, she's out there all alone, now, with maybe only six or seven, maybe eight cowhands, to run the place," Farrell said.

Dagston pulled a silver case from inside his coat pocket and removed a cigar. He bit the tip off and spit it on the floor, then lit it. He inhaled deeply and blew out a huge gray cloud.

"You forget, one of them is a redheaded kid with a fast draw," Dagston said.

"I'm faster," Farrell said, "so forget about him.

"You sure about that?"

"The next time we see him, I'll prove it."

Suddenly Curley Barnes said, for no special reason, "This sure makes it easy for the redhead to make a move on the Gavin girl, now that her pa is out of the way."

"Who's after what girl?" Dagston asked.

"The kid from Texas, the redhead, he's after the Gavin girl. Otherwise he would never have cleaned Reb's clock."

"Yeah," Tardy agreed. "I saw the way they looked at each other, all moon-faced."

Farrell smirked. "What she needs is a real man like me, not some pimply faced kid."

Dagston said, "Best be careful around here, Farrell. There's a code, people take it seriously."

Tardy chuckled. "They had a code in Shawnee Town, too, didn't they, Rice? But that didn't stop you and that fourteen-year old injin girl from doing the…"

Farrell spun around and pulled a knife from his boot and glared warningly at Tardy. "Shut your mouth about Shawnee Town, Whipple, or I'll shut it for you!"

Tardy Whipple felt the point of the knife against his throat. He nodded. "Sure, boss, sure!" Farrell put the knife back in his boot sheath.

Dagston had a worried look on his face. Things were not going the way he planned. He had lost control and now, suddenly, he felt exposed. The quicker he got rid of Rice Farrell, the better. But that wouldn't be easy. For the first time in his life, he felt fear growing inside him like a bellyache.

7.

It was in the middle of the afternoon. A trail of smoke spiraled up from the ranch house chimney, drifting and fading west on the Kansas wind. Mary Gavin came out on the front porch and stood with her hands shading her eyes, looking in the direction of Brent's Ford. She could hear the new hand, Art Haney, along with Frank and Ben, working on the corral fence, out back. Ed, who was with them, came around the yard to join her.

"Pa should have been back last night," Ed said.

Sarah and Ray Gavin came out of the house. They went up close to their mother, leaning on her. She patted Ray's head.

"What's taking him so long, momma?" Ray asked.

"I don't know, son."

"Something must have happened, ma," Sarah said. "Maybe we ought to send the hands out to look for him."

Mary Gavin nodded. "Yes, I guess so. Ed, you tell Ben and Frank to saddle up and go..." she stopped. Her eyes caught a tiny dot moving on the horizon, coming from the direction of Brent's Ford. "Hold on, I think you father's coming."

They all watched as the pin point of motion got bigger and bigger and finally turned into a buckboard with a driver and a horse in tow.

Mary Gavin's face showed no emotion. She kept her eyes fastened on the buckboard, watching it as Marshal Leach drove into the yard, made a half-circle, and stopped in front of the porch. She saw, in the back, something covered with a canvas tarp, and knew, without asking, what it was. They all knew. It spoke for itself.

The children rushed from the porch to stare with bewildered looks on their faces.

The Marshal got down, removed his hat, and went up to the porch to nod to Mary Gavin. She did not speak, but only stared at the shroud-cover body.

"I'm sorry, Mary," the Marshal said. There was a short pause. "They found Jim on the road outside of town, early this morning." All Mary Gavin could do was stare silently at the shroud. She knew if she opened her mouth to speak, her voice would crack. "It looks like he was shot and robbed by somebody."

"Ed," Mary Gavin whispered solemnly, "go get the boys."

Ed Gavin ran around the house to the corral. In a few moments he returned with Haney, Frank, and Ben. When they saw what was on the buckboard they flinched and took off their hats. Sarah and Ray began to sob. Ed looked lost.

"Boys," Mary Gavin said. "Would you take him in the house and lay him on the dining room table?" She stepped aside as Haney, Ed, Ben, and Frank lifted the shroud covered body off the buckboard and carried it in. Ray and Sarah followed.

Marshal Leach stared at Mary Gavin. "I'll find out who did this, Mary. They'll hang."

Mary Gavin nodded. "Good-day, Marshal. Thank you for bringing him home."

The Marshal knew it was time to leave. He put his hat on and untied Jim Gavin's horse. It went on its own towards the barn where the hay and oats were. Marshall Leach looked up at Mary Gavin again but she avoided his eyes. She was fighting back her tears.

"If you need me, Mary, just send one of the boys." Mary nodded. The Marshal got back on the buckboard and snapped the reins. In a moment he was out on the road back to Brent's Ford.

Ed, Haney, Ben, and Frank came out of the house and stood waiting for orders.

"Mr. Haney, I'm making you ramrod of the Lazy M." Ben and Frank nodded in agreement. It was a heavy load they didn't want on their shoulders. "I'll need two things, a casket and a grave dug up on the hill in the family plot. And let me know when they're both finished. Ed will show you where the lumber is."

They all went out back to the barn. Ben and Frank got the shovels and left Ed and Haney to build the casket.

"Sorry about your dad," Haney said.

Ed wiped his eyes. "This has Dagston's hand all over it. I want that bastard dead!"

"Best leave it to the Marshal," Haney said.

51

"Marshal Leach?" Ed forced a sad chuckled. "He doesn't know his ass from his elbow!"

They got out the tools they needed and went to work. Two hours later the casket, its cover, and a cross were completed. They took everything, over to the house, into the dining room. The women had wrapped Jim Gavin's body in a green, felt, blanket, and sewn it tight.

When Ben and Frank came down from the hill, the four hands carefully placed Jim Gavin's body into the casket. After they had nailed the top on, Mary Gavin got the family Bible. They followed her out of the house and across the yard.

It was almost sundown by then. The wind was stirring up little clouds of red dust as they made their way up the hillside to the Gavin's family plot where several generations of Jim Gavin's people were buried. There were weeds on the plots. Some of the wooden crosses were weathered and warped.

Haney, Ed, Frank, and Ben used two ropes to lower the casket down into the hole. They dropped the ropes in too. They then stood aside and waited as Mary Gavin read several selections from Psalms. When she was finished, Sarah sang,

"Amazing Grace." Her voice was strong and clear and the wind carried it down the hill to the yard.

Just as Sarah was finished, they heard a high-pitched sound from the corral. It was Jim Gavin's horse making a mournful bawling sound that the wind caught and carried up to them.

"When you're finished, you boys come down for coffee and pie," Mary Gavin said. She nodded. Sarah and Ray followed her back towards the house. The wind was whispering in the pines on the hillside. It followed them down, blowing and snapping at their hair, and Sarah's dress.

Ed, Frank, Ben, and Art Haney took turns filling in Jim Gavin's grave. They pounded the wooden cross in the ground at its head then slowly went down the hill for coffee and the best apple pie this side of the Missouri Brakes.

8.

A few days after Jim Gavin's death, Dagston, Farrell, Curley, and Tardy, were sitting at a back table in the C-D Saloon drinking and talking strategy.

"So, what if she still won't sell?" Dagston said. "Then what?"

Farrell was ready for that. "Me and my boys will go up to their line-camp shack and scare off a few of her cowpokes. The rest will go running. When the word gets around how dangerous it is out there, nobody will work for her."

"And if that doesn't do it?" Dagston fretted.

"Then we poison the water," Farrell said.

"You can't," Dagston said. "It's running water, a stream. You can't poison a running stream, can you?"

"Sure."

"Yeah? How?" Dagston didn't believe it.

"You pick a spot up stream and toss in some dead, animals. You fix it so they don't float away."

"Maybe we should have done that with Gavin's body," Tardy Whipple chuckled.

"That's stupid," Dagston said. "You'd be poisoning half the cattle in the area."

"Who cares?" Farrell snickered. They all started laughing except for Dagston.

Charley came over from the bar and approached his boss. "What is it?" Dagston asked.

The bartender pointed to a man in a blue, ill-fitting suit and city shoes and hat, standing next to a large carpetbag, at the bar.

"A salesman?" Dagston asked. "Get rid of him. We aren't buying."

"No, boss," Charley said, "this guy just got out of Kansas State Penitentiary, and is looking for the redhead. He says he knows Sidewinder Smith."

They all stared at the man for a moment before Dagston got up and said, "Boys, let's check this fellow out."

Dagston went up front with Farrell close on his heels. Curley and Tardy went to the far end, while Charley took his place behind the bar, looking on.

"My name is Cleet Dagston. I own the place. I understand you're looking for Art Haney."

"That's right. Do you know where I can find him?"

"Why yes, as a matter of fact I do, mister."

"Janeen. Tom Janeen."

"He's working out at the Lazy M ranch, Mr. Janeen."

Janeen chuckled. "Are you sure that's Haney? From what Sidewinder told me, the kid hates work."

"So you know Sidewinder Smith, do you, friend?" Farrell said.

"Yeah, we were cell mates until a week ago," Janeen said.

"Oh, really?" Dagston said, as if he didn't fully believe it.

"Yeah. He asked me to look up his nephew," Janeen said. "The kid working doesn't sound right. Sidewinder said the kid was a card sharp. Made a living off cards."

"Well, I offered him a good legitimate job, but he turned it down," Dagston said. "Maybe you could talk some sense into his young head. Working at the Lazy M is a dead end job."

"I might do that, Mr. Dagston," Janeen said.

"If you do, I'll be very grateful." Dagston said. "So grateful, in fact, that you'll never have to buy a drink again at the C-D Saloon, sir."

Janeen whistled. "Now that's what I call a hard to refuse offer, sir! I'd be on my way out to the Lazy M right now, except that I came here by rail. I don't have a horse."

"That's not a problem, Mr. Janeen," Dagston said. "You just come with me, sir."

Tom Janeen picked up his carpetbag. He followed Dagston outside. They went up the road towards the jailhouse. Farrell walked alongside Janeen, staring at him.

"You fast with a gun, Janeen?" He asked.

"Me? Oh, sure," Janeen chuckled. "I'm the fastest draw in the west, mister."

Farrell didn't like that answer, but let it go. "You're not totting a gun. How come?"

"That would be a parole violation," Janeen said.

"What if I gave you a gun and we had it out?"

"Parole violation, too."

"But you'd be dead, so they couldn't jail you, could they?"

Janeen laughed. "Good point, sir. Good point."

"Oh, by the way, my name is Rice Farrell. Maybe you've heard of me? I out drew Scotty Ferguson in Renson City, last year."

"Oh, yes! So, that was you? Congratulations, Mr. Farrell," Janeen chuckled. "You killed a half-blind, sixty-year old scoundrel who couldn't find his ass in a windstorm!"

"Why you!"

Dagston burst out laughing. Farrell was just about to grab Janeen by the arm when the Marshal came up behind them.

"We were just looking for you Marshal Leach," Dagston said. He patted the Marshal on the back. Before the Marshal could answer, Dagston went on with, "This is Mr. Janeen. He's looking for Art Haney. I was hoping you might be able to take him out to the Lazy M."

"Sure, I was going to pay Mrs. Gavin a visit to see how she's holding up, anyhow. I'd be glad to, Mr. Dagston."

The Marshal shook Tom Janeen's hand. Dagston and Farrell left, walking back to the C-D Saloon.

"Where you from, Janeen?" the Marshal asked, as they hitched up the buckboard.

"Just got out of the state pen," Janeen said.

The Marshal gave Janeen a skeptical look. "You serious?"

"Very serious," Janeen said. "Just did ten years for robbing trains. Graduated with honors."

The Marshal chuckled. "I guess you weren't very good at it, were you? Robbing trains?"

"Not good enough, Marshal," Janeen said.

"Did you learn your lesson?"

"Indeed I did. Indeed I did."

When they finished hitching the horse they got into the buckboard and headed west in the direction of the Lazy M. Brent's Ford was soon far behind them. They were quiet for a while as Tom Janeen studied the landscape.

"Jim Gavin, the owner, was killed last week," Marshal Leach said. "We found his body on the road, right about here. It had three bullet holes. One in the heart, and one on each side of the chest." The Marshal stopped the buckboard and pointed. "So, be extra sensitive when you get out to the Lazy M."

"When did it happen?"

"At night. Both Gavin and his killer were up in the saddle, most likely. He was going home and someone ambushed and robbed him."

"Shot him three times, huh?"

"Yep. The chest shots were a waste of lead."

"Did you get the bullets out?"

"Oh, yeah. The town doctor, Doc Sloan, who is also the undertaker, used to be a coroner's assistant. He just loves to dig around in people's bodies," the Marshal said. "I told him to dig away."

Janeen thought for a while. "Say, Marshal, you ever hear of a sawdust box?"

"Nope, what's a sawdust box?"

"Well, say I dug three slugs out of a body, like you did Gavin's body. And say I suspect one or more people of his murder."

"Go on."

"I get those people to fire their guns into the sawdust box and see if the slugs from their guns match the slugs dug out of Gavin's body. Do you suspect one or three people of murdering Jim Gavin, Marshal?"

Marshal Leach started the buckboard moving again. He seemed to be thinking deep thoughts. "A sawdust box, huh? Where did you come up with that?"

"I did a lot of reading in prison, Marshal," Janeen said. "Mostly about crime. I wanted to know what the police knew."

The Marshal laughed. "You're not so dumb, Janeen."

"Oh, and I hope you don't think I'm trying to tell you your job, but…"

"But what?"

"Another hobby of mine when I was in the pen was to study criminal characteristics, the working mind of the criminal. There were lots of books on that in the library, there."

"And?"

"Where's Mr. Dagston from?"

"Out east. Chicago, I think. Why?"

"Did he come into town with a bundle of money?"

"Yeah, he sure did. He's got plenty, why?"

"Ever wonder where or how he came by all that ready cash?"

"Nope. He gave me this job when I was down and out, so I owe him a lot," the Marshal said.

"Don't get mad, but he acts like he owns you and the whole town, Marshal. That's an awful lot of power for one man," Janeen said. "It wouldn't hurt to send a wire to Chicago, just to see if his name pops up for something."

"Something like what?"

"Bank embezzlement, fraud, maybe?"

"Are you joking, Janeen?"

"Not really," Janeen said. "It has happened before."

"Look Mr. Dagston is an upstanding citizen who has done a whole lot for Brent's Ford. He really has…"

"I'm sure he has, but…" Janeen stopped there and shrugged.

The Marshal chuckled. "You sure are a suspicious cuss, Mr. Janeen."

But as they traveled along in silence, Janeen's words began to weigh heavily on the Marshal's mind.

9.

The Marshal and Tom Janeen were just coming up to the Lazy M when they saw a man ride furiously out of the yard with an angry look on his face. He passed them without so much as a glance, a wave, or a nod, and disappeared into the distance in a cloud of dust.

"Somebody scalded that dog," Janeen said, chuckling.

"I guess Mrs. Gavin is in an ill humor, today," the Marshal said. "We'd better tread easy."

The Marshal drove the buckboard into the yard. He stopped near the porch where Mary Gavin stood. She had a very annoyed look on her face. Janeen grabbed his carpetbag, and he and he marshal got down. They took off their hats.

"That was the third one in as many days," Mary Gavin said. "Now, all of a sudden every cowboy in Kansas wants to un-widow me, Marshal."

The Marshal chuckled. "Word gets around fast, Mary."

"That one wanted to join the Lazy M with the Leaning-T in holy matrimony," she chuckled. "Oh, sorry, how are you these days, Marshal?"

"I'm fine, Mary," Marshal Leach said, "just fine."

Suddenly Mary noticed the man next to the Marshal. She immediately mistook him for another suitor. He seemed to be leering salaciously at her in a vulgar way, as if he was mentally peeling her clothes off. It was bold and offensive to her. It made her feel naked. She crossed her arms defensively.

"What are you gawking at, mister? Never seen a woman wearing men's clothing before?"

The Marshal stepped back, happy to watch the fireworks.

"Ma'am," Tom Janeen said, "I was just wondering what's under the shirt and pants."

"Well, you're never going to find that out are you, so stop wondering," Mary said.

"I was also wondering how beautiful you'd look in one of them pink, low cut, strapless dresses I seen in a catalogue."

"You're not ever going to find that out either, mister, are you?"

"I wouldn't bet on it, ma'am."

"Maybe I should just come down there and slap your face!"

"I would be honored if you were to do that Mrs. Gavin," Janeen said with a smile.

"What's your name, friend," Mary asked.

"Janeen, ma'am. Tom Janeen."

"Well, Mr. Janeen, tell me what you see when you look at me, sir," Mary said.

Janeen stopped to consider the question for a moment, not knowing exactly how to answer it. It sounded like some kind of trap.

"Well, ma'am, since you asked, on the surface I see a woman who has been hit hard by life. A woman who can take it and throw it right back. A woman who is nobody's fool and…"

Mary Gavin cut Tom Janeen off. "You know what I see, from here, Mr. Janeen?"

"No, ma'am, but I think I'm going to find, out right quick!"

"I see a man in a prison suit. That's all I see. A man with a weak back and soft hands who couldn't make it in life doing an honest day's work," Mary said. "So, Mr. Janeen, you just climb back up on that buckboard and go back to wherever you came from. I'm not interested."

Marshal Leach broke out laughing.

"What's so funny, Marshal?" Mary Gavin asked.

"You two arguing like a couple of school kids, and you don't even know each other. Now, just relax and calm down, Mary. Mr. Janeen is not here to court you. No, he's here to see the new man, Art Haney."

"Oh, dear," Mary said. "I feel like such a fool. My apologies, sir."

"No, ma'am. I'm the one who should apologize. I'm truly sorry for gawking, but what I said about your beauty still holds. You have my admiration, and respect ma'am."

The Marshal chuckled, smiling. "I enjoyed the give and take myself, but I'll be going now, Mary. I just wanted to see if you were okay, and I see that you are. Don't be too hard on Mr. Janeen. I'm thinking about considering him as a friend."

"Then I will be gentle with him, Marshal. Good-day."

The Marshal got up on the buckboard and was soon lost behind a cloud of dust. There was an awkward moment. Tom Janeen looked around.

"Nice spread you have here, Mrs. Gavin."

"You haven't spent much time on a ranch, have you, Mr. Janeen?" He liked the way she said his name.

"Ah, not really."

"Robbed banks, did you?"

"Trains."

"Got caught?"

"Actually no. The railroad put out an amnesty offer. Ten years and a clean start. I did my ten."

"And now?" Mary Gavin asked. Tom Janeen shrugged. "You must have given it some thought, during those ten years."

"Ah, yes. Believe it or not, I was thinking of going to work for the law. You have my permission to laugh, ma'am, but it's true."

"Oh, no," Mary said. "I hear the Pinkertons hire ex-cons like you." Janeen flinched. "I'm sorry, I meant…"

There was another awkward moment. Janeen said, "Ah, Art Haney, ma'am?"

"Yes, you'll find him out back with my oldest boy, Ed and the rest, probably around the stables or barn."

Janeen nodded. He put his hat on, picked up his carpetbag, and went around the house. He stopped a few yards from the corral fence. He saw four cowboys replacing rotted fence posts.

"Which one of you is Art Haney?"

Haney stopped working and turned around. He looked at Janeen for a moment. "I'm Haney."

"Could we talk in private?"

"Who are you?" Haney put down his shovel.

"I'm Tom Janeen. I knew your uncle."

69

"Well, I got no secrets from my friends," Haney said. "So, say what you have to say."

Tom Janeen put his carpetbag down and reached into it and took out a large, brown envelope. It was sealed. He handed it to the redhead.

"Your uncle said to give you this, kid," Janeen said.

Haney took the envelope. Janeen picked up the carpetbag. He walked away. Haney, Ed, Ben, and Frank watched until he was out of sight before Haney opened the envelope. He pulled out a bankbook, some official looking papers, and a letter. As he read the letter, he shook his head in disbelief. He handed it to Ed. Ed read it and handed it to Ben and Frank.

"We can't read," Ben said. "What does it say?" He handed it back to Ed.

"It says Haney is rich, that's what it says! He got a deed to a house in El Paso, Texas, and five-thousand in the bank!"

"Horse shit!" Frank said.

"No horse shit," Ed said. "It's all here. The deed, the bank book, the letter! Come on, Haney! We gotta show this to my mom!"

70

Ed and the redhead went quickly through the back door, into the kitchen. They showed the letter and the rest of the stuff to Mary Gavin. She looked it over slowly and carefully.

"Well, it's all in order. Notarized and all Mr. Haney. It appears you have suddenly become a rich man."

Haney looked over at Sarah Gavin and smiled. Mary Gavin noticed the attraction between the two.

"Mr. Haney," Mary said, "if you want, I'll lock this up in the safe until you leave."

"Leave?" Sarah was concerned.

"Well, you don't think Mr. Haney will want to spend the rest of his life working on a ranch now, do you, Sarah? I'm sure he'll want to be leaving for El Paso as soon as he can."

Art Haney looked conflicted. He wanted to stay and wanted to leave, at the same time.

"Well, I'm in no rush, ma'am," Haney said. "A few more days, even a week or so more, won't matter. It'll be there when I get there, won't it?"

"Of course, Mr. Haney, of course," Mary said. "You're more than welcome to stay as long as you want to." Sarah gave a sigh of relief. "Ah, where is Mr. Janeen?"

71

"He took off," Ed said. "He headed out for parts unknown, I guess."

"Well, you go get him," Mary insisted "You should have offered him our hospitality, at least, Ed Gavin."

"I'll do it," Art Haney said. He went out the door, running. He caught up with Tom Janeen fifty yards from the house.

"Mrs. Gavin wants you back at the house," Haney said. He grabbed the carpetbag from Janeen. "Anyway, you look like you're about to collapse from hunger. You like apple pie?"

"Does a bear have balls? Sure. I love apple pie."

"Well, this is apple pie heaven."

They walked slowly back up the road towards the ranch. "How's my uncle doing?"

"He's dying."

Haney looked away for a moment. He cleared his throat. "Sorry to hear that."

"Yeah, me too. I'm going to miss the old coot. We robbed a lot of trains together."

"You're not doing that anymore, are you?"

"No, I can't. I've had enough of that."

"Looking to settle down, huh?"

"Maybe."

"We sure could use another hand here."

"See these, kid?" Janeen said, holding his hands up for inspection.

"Yeah, I see them. So what?"

"What do you think these hands are good for?"

"Cards and killin'?"

"That's right. Cards and killing. They wouldn't be much good on a ranch."

"Well, I got a strong feelin' that killin' is gonna come to the Lazy M pretty darn soon."

"Oh, really? Dagston and Farrell?"

"You guessed it, friend."

They walked in silence for a moment. "That apple pie? Is it really that good?"

"It's better than good!" Art Haney said.

"Then let's have at it."

Art Haney, alias the Pecos Kid, had the answer he was hoping for.

10.

"Mr. Janeen, why don't you stay in the bunkhouse with the boys until you decide what you're going to do?" Mary Gavin asked her guest, after the evening meal. They were sitting on the porch and Janeen was rolling a cigarette.

Janeen nodded and smiled. "Thank you, ma'am, but I think I'd only be in the way."

He gazed out across the yard towards the distant hills that looked purple in the evening dusk. It was quiet except for the natural sounds of nature all around them.

Mary was just about to say something when they heard hoof beats off in the distance, coming towards the house. They listened and in a few minutes a rider came tearing into the yard, pulling up short in a cloud of dust.

"Ken! What in the blazes!"

The man called Ken took off his hat and looked back the way he had come. He stared at Janeen for a moment, then back to Mary Gavin.

"I'm finished, Mrs. Gavin. Could I have my pay now?"

"Your pay? What in tarnation is going on, Ken?"

Three more riders came pounding up alongside Ken. They stopped to dismount and also stood staring nervously back in the direction they had come.

"Tim! Gil! Roy! What happened? Why aren't you all up at the line-camp?" By now, Art Haney, Frank, and Ben had come from the bunkhouse. Ed, Ray, and Sarah came from the kitchen. They all stood staring at the cowboys.

"Somebody is taking pot shots at us, Mrs. Gavin, and they're keeping it up, day and night. The cattle is scattered to kingdom come, all hell has broken loose up there!" Gil said. He removed his sombrero and showed her where a bullet had gone through. "That one was too close for comfort, ma'am!"

Mary looked at Tom Janeen. "It's Dagston." Then, to the cowboys, "Alright boys. Come on in and I'll give you your wages. Thank God none of you got hurt."

In half an hour they were paid and back on their horses.

"I'm sorry, Mrs. Gavin, but…" Ken started to say.

"It's alright, Ken, I understand. Good-luck. And don't stop at Brent's Ford. This is Dagston's doing. He's hired some gunslingers," Mary said. They nodded. She watched them ride off.

"I guess things are changing," Ed said. "It used to be when you signed on to work for a brand you fought for that brand, too."

"I don't want anyone killed over some cattle, son," Mary Gavin said. "Especially ours..." Her voice trailed off and faded as the impact of what was happening hit her.

"What are we gonna do, momma?" Sarah asked, concerned.

"We'll just have to figure something out," her mother said.

Art Haney said, "If you need money, my five-thousand is at your disposal, ma'am."

"Thank you, Mr. Haney. If I do, I'll pay you back."

There didn't seem to be much else to say. Haney, Ben, and Frank went down to the bunkhouse and the children went back into the kitchen, leaving Mary Gavin and Tom Janeen alone on the porch.

"So you think it's Dagston, Mrs. Gavin?"

"Oh, it's Dagston, alright. He's been after the Lazy M for a long time, now, Mr. Janeen. And I damn well know he had a hand in my husband's murder."

Janeen nodded. "Say, ma'am, you wouldn't mind if I hung around here for a while, would you?"

"No, but this isn't where you'd want to be, I'd think, Mr. Janeen. What with all my troubles."

Janeen chuckled. "Trouble? I feel right at home with trouble, ma'am. In fact, I've been known to stir up a little trouble, myself, now and then."

Before she could answer, Janeen walked down the porch steps into the yard. "Ma'am, I'll be down in the bunkhouse, if you need me." He tipped his hat and walked off.

Mary Gavin stared after this strange man, wondering what he was all about, who he really was, and why she was attracted to him and found his presence comforting.

The next morning, Sarah told her mother she needed to go into town to Price's Mercantile for some cloth for a new dress she wanted to make. Mary got out the buckboard and along with Ray, and Sarah headed east for Brent's Ford.

As they came into town, Dagston and Farrell watched them from the porch of the C-D Saloon. Mary snapped the reins. As she went quickly by, she heard Farrell laughing and making a rude remark. Once at the mercantile they hurried in, got the cloth, and started back for the Lazy M. They came abreast of the saloon when Dagston jumped out into the road and grabbed the horse's halter. He brought the buckboard to a sudden, jolting stop.

Rice Farrell smiled at Sarah from the porch, trying to get her attention. She looked away, to avoid his suggestive stare.

"Mrs. Gavin," Dagston said, "we have to talk."

"There's nothing to talk about, sir!"

"Look, I'll give you ten-dollars an acre, Mrs. Gavin," Dagston said. "And that's my final offer."

"Why that's ridiculous! You offered my husband twenty-dollars an acre!"

"Your husband is gone now, Mrs. Gavin," Dagston said. "Think about the safety of your children."

"Is that a threat, sir?"

"The whole town knows about your husband and Nelly Tulley, Mrs. Gavin," Dagston said. "Why don't you just sell and go where people won't call you a fool?"

"For the last time, get out of my way!"

"Do you know Nelly Tulley is a whore, Mrs. Gavin?"

Mary Gavin cracked the reins and yelled, "Yaa!" as loud as she could. The horse reared and lurched forward. Dagston spun around off balance and fell sideways. There was a crunching sound as the wheels of the buckboard ran over his left ankle.

Curley Barnes and Tardy Whipple came rushing up and got Dagston on his feet. He glared hatefully after the buckboard which, by then, was at the edge of town.

"Did you see that? The crazy woman ran me over! Call the Marshal! No, get me over to Doc Sloan's place."

Further out on the road, Mary Gavin slowed the rig down to a gentle gait.

"I'm going to have to kill him, momma," little Ray said. "He wasn't nice to you."

"It's alright, son. Let it be."

"He lied about daddy, didn't he momma?" Sarah said uncertainly. "Didn't he?"

"No, baby, I've known for a long time. But I guess I can't blame your daddy, what with my shirt, pants and boots. Men like pretty faces with makeup, and fancy dresses."

They all sat quietly after that, lost in their own thoughts.

An hour later, back in town, Cleet Dagston, using a cane, came limping into the C-D Saloon. He stopped at the bar. Charley poured him a whiskey. He drank it fast and had another. A moment later Rice Farrell came from the back room.

"How's the ankle?"

"Bad, but it's not broken." Dagston groaned in pain.

"I told you she'd be a big problem," Farrell said.

"She won't listen to reason. I don't know what to do."

"I do," Farrell said. "No more being nice to her. Now it's time to get rough, like I did with her old man."

"You don't mean kill her, do you?"

81

"I'm for taking them all out. Hell, I could get ten drunken gunnies for ten-bucks a night to do it. Just one night's work, and all your problems will be solved."

Dagston sneered. "Yeah, just like you solved my problems with Gavin! No thanks, that's going too far. They have children out there."

"Give me three-hundred bucks."

"What for?" Dagston grimaced. The pain was getting more intense. He looked disoriented and confused.

"You don't need to know. Just give it to me and forget you did. Go to sleep and by tomorrow all your problems with the Lazy M will be gone. It will be as if they never existed!"

Dagston sighed. He felt too weak to fight Farrell any more, and the pain in his ankle was getting more unbearable each moment. He called Charley over. "Give Mr. Farrell whatever he asks. I'm going to my office. My ankle is killing me. I don't want to see anyone until morning."

Dagston left the saloon and limped over to his office. He sat at his desk and pulled a bottle of whiskey from a drawer and started drinking straight from the bottle.

"Damn your rotten hide, Farrell! You're destroying me!" Dagston whined.

After a while he went into the backroom and laid on his cot. He had a strange, scary feeling that his whole life was about to unravel, and he could do nothing to stop it.

He fell asleep cursing the day he had ever met Jim Gavin or Rice Farrell.

11.

It was nightfall, and pitch black under an overcast sky. Haney, Ben, and Frank were at the bunkhouse table playing cards under the dull glow of a hanging kerosene lamp. Tom Janeen sat on a bunk, off to one side, in the shadows, listening to the brave talk between Ben and Frank. They wanted to go up to the line-shack and fight it out. Art Haney detached himself from them and went and sat next to Janeen.

Suddenly the bunkhouse door swung open. Curley Barnes stood there looking in at them. He had a worried look on his face. Ben and Frank remembered him from the day when Farrell had shot Earl.

"What the hell do you want?" Ben growled.

"We ought to kick your ass!" Frank said.

"I'm on my way to Texas," Barnes said, "and I just wanted to let you know that Rice Farrell is gonna' ambush you ass holes right around midnight, when you're all drunk and fast asleep. And if I were you, I'd keep a close eye on the Gavin girl. "Bye-bye, suckers!"

Before anyone could react, Curley Barnes had disappeared into the night.

Haney and Janeen stood up. They stared at each other, a concerned look on their faces.

"Looks like this is the trouble you've been expecting, kid. I guess it's time to separate the men from the boys."

The redhead chuckled. "Hell, we ain't got enough men here to fight our way out of a paper bag!"

"Yeah. It does look tight, doesn't it, kid?" Janeen said.

Haney turned to Ben and Frank.

"Okay," he said. "It looks like we're in for it. If any of you two want out, you'd best go right now." No one moved. "Any of you two ever shot a man, before?" No one said a word. Haney swore. "Any of you every shot a deer or a buff?" They both nodded.

"Well, that's somethin'," Haney said, trying to sound confident. He knew they were in trouble. Ben and Frank looked scared.

"Look," Janeen said to the two cowhands, "you two should know that Farrell might come at us with fifteen, maybe twenty men. All he had to do was go down to the railhead in Brent's Ford where the low life's and drunks hang out. If he wanted to, he could come up with thirty crazies, easy, if he had the money."

"You sure you two are ready for this? It sure might get messy," Haney said. "You two can ride out and nobody will hold it against you."

Ben cleared his throat and said, "I'm scared, Haney, I won't lie about that. But Mrs. Gavin has treated me like a son. I'll fight for the Lazy M."

Frank just shrugged, not saying anything.

Haney stood quiet for a moment, trying to get a handle on the situation. Finally he spoke.

"Frank," Haney said, "you have to sneak into town and tell the Marshal." Frank nodded. "And don't let anybody see you, and stay clear of the road! Got that?"

"Yeah," Frank said, "sure."

"Go out real casual like, and sneak over to the barn and saddle up," Haney said. "It's darker than a well-digger's ass out there, so nobody will see you. Go easy until you get on the road and then ride like the devil!"

Frank put on his gun belt and pulled his sombrero down over his face and eased out into the night.

Haney looked at Ben. "You think he'll do it or will he ride on? He didn't look so good, kind of scared."

Ben shrugged. "If he says he'll do it, he'll do it, Haney. He's my pard."

Haney turned to Janeen. "Why don't you go up to the house and tell them what's going on, and then come back here."

"Right," Janeen said. "It must be close to midnight. Before I go put out the light, like we're going to sleep."

"Good idea," Haney said. He blew the lantern out.

Janeen went out into the night. The side window of the house, near the kitchen, was lit up. He could see Ed and Ray moving around. Keeping to the shadows, Janeen went slowly over to the back porch and in through the kitchen door.

Inside, at the kitchen table, Mary and Sarah sat before a sewing machine, working on her new dress. Mary looked up, surprised.

"Ma'am," Janeen said, "do you have a moment?"

"Can't it wait until morning, Mr. Janeen?"

"Ah, I'm afraid not."

"Well, what is it, then," Mary said. She sounded tired. She yawned sleepily.

"Ma'am, Rice Farrell is coming to pay us a visit tonight, right about midnight?" Janeen paused. "And he's bringing about twenty-five of his friends along with him?"

Everyone froze in place. "Are you quite sure, Mr. Janeen?"

"Reasonably sure, ma'am, yes."

"What do you advise me to do, Mr. Janeen?"

"We're probably being watched right now, so just act normal," Janeen said. "I'm going to leave, and after I do, put all the lights out in the house. Have Sarah and Ray hide someplace. Ed and you should arm yourselves. Don't leave the house unless it's absolutely necessary."

"It sounds serious."

"It is, Mrs. Gavin, very serious." Janeen went out the door. "Good-night, ma'am," he said loudly. By the time he was close to the bunkhouse, the ranch house was dark.

Haney met him at the bunkhouse door. He handed him a rifle and a box of shells. Ben came out well armed. He followed Haney and Janeen over to the corral fence. It was coal-black in the shadows. They could just barely see the bunkhouse fifty feet away. The three of them spread out along the corral fence in a line, with the extra ammunition in their pockets and their rifles at the ready. They hunkered down and waited.

Time seemed to move slowly. The horses had gone into the barn to stay warm. Coyotes howled up in the hills and beyond. Bats flew by, just above their head, curious about what was going on.

Finally, it started.

They heard the sound of rocks falling as someone scrambled down the hill behind the bunkhouse. Soon black silhouettes came around to the door. There were about eight of them. They spread out. One of them opened the door as another one lit a kerosene lamp and tossed it in. The bunkhouse burst into flames.

"Wake up you jackasses!" One of them yelled drunkenly.

They stood back, firing through the door, walls, and windows of the bunkhouse. They shouted and laughed like crazed, drunken marauders.

Haney and Janeen were the first to fire back, dropping two of the eight. As they did so, a volley of bullets came from above and behind them. They were caught in a crossfire. The remaining men at the bunkhouse scattered and took up firing positions. Laying low, they started firing over at the corral fence while those up above fired down at it, trying to pin Haney, Janeen, and Ben down.

One attacker started towards the house. He was cut down by a shotgun blast from inside. The Gavins were ready for what was to come.

The bunkhouse was now up in flames. The light exposed both the attackers and the defenders at the corral fence. Janeen shot down two of five of Farrell's men as they came down the hill behind them, in an attempt to outflank the trio. Three got into the barn but didn't show themselves.

"Those drunken idiots, they're going to burn the barn down!" Ben yelled.

Suddenly the hayloft in the barn went up in flames. Both horses and men came running out.

"Into the house!" Janeen screamed, making a mad dash across the yard towards the back porch.

Bullets followed him all the way as Janeen went flying in and under the kitchen table. Art Haney was right behind, along with Ben. They could hear Ed and Mary Gavin firing shotguns from the windows in the living room.

"You and Haney stay here, in case they try to come in this way," Janeen said. He belly-crawled into the living room and up to a window.

Two men were making a run towards the front porch. They were easy to see in the light of the burning bunkhouse. Janeen took out one and Ed took out the other. Mary Gavin took out a third that came sneaking up from the road.

A few more of Farrell's men came down the hill behind the bunkhouse and joined their friends. They rushed the front yard screaming insanely.

"I'm sorry momma," Ed said, as he shot down one more. He was crying hard. His body shook. He had never killed a man before.

"It's alright, son," Mary Gavin said.

"Will God forgive me, momma?"

"God always forgives, son."

Six more gunnies came out of the shadows into the yard. They seemed drunk, and that made it all the worse. It took several hits to knock them down as they poured lead into the house. Window glass flew everywhere, showering down on the defenders. Some slugs went right through the house wall.

Janeen crawled over and flipped the dining room table. He dragged it to the window for a shield. It worked fine and they were able to pour shots into the front yard at will.

After a while there was a lull in the fighting. All of a sudden they heard Haney and Ben firing from the kitchen.

"They're coming at the back," Janeen said. "I hope the kid can hold them." He screamed into the kitchen. "You guys need help?"

"Ben's dead!" Haney screamed.

Janeen crawled into the kitchen just as the door gave way and three men crashed in. Haney dropped his rifle and drew his Colt and fanned off three shots, dropping them in the doorway, in a pile. Janeen fired three shots through the open doorway, into the back yard. He heard one man fall and another gasp in pain as if hit.

Suddenly he heard Mary Gavin and Ed firing rapid fire into the yard. He scrambled back into the dining room and up to the window. At least ten men were making a rush at the front of the house, firing a deadly fusillade. Janeen, Mary, and Ed crouched down behind the table, feeling the oncoming slugs pounding against it. Wooden splinters went flying around the room.

"I'm out of shells," Mary Gavin said.

"Yeah, me, too," Janeen said.

Suddenly they heard the distant thunder of horses. The bullets stopped for a moment and Janeen got on his knees and look out towards the road.

"It's the Marshal!" he yelled.

Marshal Leach, Frank, and four riders came into the front yard firing. Several of the attackers fell dead, while some threw up their arms in surrender. Those in the back of the house scattered and ran up the hill. A few of those were knocked off before they reached the top. Finally the shooting stopped. There were only five attackers left alive. They were herded together and their hands tied behind their backs.

The Marshal looked around at the carnage. Bodies lay everywhere. The barn and bunkhouse burned like torches in the night.

"What in God's name happened here, folks?" Marshal Leech asked as Mary, Ed, and Janeen came out of the house.

"Dagston's man, Rice Farrell, paid us a visit Marshal," Mary said.

Frank came over to join them. "Where's Ben?" he asked.

"He's in the kitchen." Ed said, sobbing.

Haney came out through the front door just as Frank rushed up. The redhead had a slight bullet wound along his right cheek. Frank stopped and stared at him.

"Where's Ben?" Frank asked. He saw the look on Haney's face.

"He didn't make it," Haney said solemnly. Frank ran into the house yelling Ben's name. Haney shook his head sadly as he went down the porch steps into the yard to face Mary Gavin. "I'm sorry, Mrs. Gavin. Ben is dead."

Mary choked back her tears and patted Art Haney on the shoulder. "It's not your doing. I'm laying it all on Farrell and Dagston's head, Mr. Haney."

"God," the Marshal said, "it's a miracle any one of you are alive! I never saw anything like this in all my years! Where's Sarah and Ray? I don't see them."

Suddenly Mary yelled, "The children!"

At that moment, Ray came out of the house. He stood on the porch crying, looking terrified.

"Where's your sister?" Mary asked.

"That man took her!" Ray cried.

12.

It took the Marshal two days to organize a group of volunteers from the surrounding ranches to clean up the mess at the Lazy M ranch. News about the fight had spread like wildfire and it came to be called, "The Lazy M Massacre." The dead were taken into town to be identified and the survivors to the jailhouse to be charged.

One of the survivors spilled the beans on Farrell. He told the Marshal that Farrell was taking the Gavin girl out to his hideaway in a place called the Devil's Den. The Marshal passed that information on to Mary Gavin the next day.

"I never heard of the place, Mary, have you?" the Marshal asked.

"No, Marshal, I never have."

"I have," Tom Janeen said. "A long time ago, when they called me Kid Janeen. That's where I first met Sidewinder."

"Where is it?" the Marshal asked.

"It's west of Cheneyville, in the outback badlands," Janeen said. "It's where wanted men hide out. A lawmen won't go there, if he's smart."

"Well, if that's where it is, it's way out of my jurisdiction," the Marshal said, shaking his head.

There wasn't much left of the Lazy M ranch, just the main house. The bunkhouse was a pile of ashes, and almost all of the barn was gone. Luckily, the horses had gotten out and most of the saddles and riding gear survived. A day later, the horses came back looking to be fed and watered. The only cowhands left were Frank and Haney, so Mary gave Tom Janeen and them the extra bedrooms in the ranch house as well as run of the kitchen.

The fight did something to young Ed Gavin. He had never killed a man before, and it lay heavy on his mind. He stayed in his room and wouldn't come out to talk or eat. He finally let Tom Janeen in.

"Look, son," Janeen said, "I know what you're going through. I went through it myself and so did Art Haney. But if you hadn't killed those men, they would have killed you and done bad things to your mother and sister. You fought for them and they're proud of you. And so am I."

97

"But I feel like I did something bad and God hates me."

"You ever read the Bible? The Old Testament?"

"No, why?"

"Well, you read it while we're gone. Count how many times God ordered his people to kill their enemies, and blessed them for it."

"He did?"

"Yep. It's all there, in the Good Book, son."

Ed Gavin dried his eyes and stood up. "I'm hungry."

"Go see you mom," Janeen said. "She'll rustle you up some grub."

The next day, Tom Janeen and Mary Gavin saw Art Haney out in the yard saddling his horse. They went out to watch him.

"Going someplace, kid?" Janeen asked.

"Yeah, I'm going after Sarah."

"You going alone, or can I tag along too, seeing as I'm the only one who knows where the Devil's Den is."

"You don't have a horse, friend," Haney said. "So I don't see how that can happen."

"Yes he does," Mary said. "He can take the big stallion. It'll carry two."

"Oh, okay Janeen. You're in, I guess."

"How about me?" Mary Gavin asked. "Aren't I invited to this shindig?"

"Ah, ma'am, women don't go willingly to the Devil's Den. And those that do, don't fare well there. They become community property, if you know what I mean.

"If I don't go Mr. Janeen, then I'm afraid you'll have to walk all the way there."

Janeen chuckled. "I get your drift, ma'am. I stand corrected, you are invited."

"As I expected to be."

"We'll need a packhorse," Janeen said, "and enough food for about a week, maybe longer."

"But, why not just take a buckboard, instead of a packhorse?" Mary asked.

"The land out there is too rough," Janeen said, "and a buckboard will only slow us down." Mary Gavin nodded.

Frank, Ed, and Ray came out into the yard to see what was going on.

"Frank," Mary said. "We're going after Sarah. You'll be in charge while we're gone. When the Marshal comes, tell him where we went. Ed, Ray, you boys help Frank, and don't give him a hard time, you hear?" The boys nodded.

Early the following morning Mary Gavin and Art Haney stood in the yard in front of the house holding the reins of their mounts. One end of a lead-rope was tied around the packhorse's halter, and the other end was tied to the back of Mary's saddle. She also held the reins of her husband's big black stallion horse. It pawed the ground with one hoof, anxious to get moving.

"What's he doing in there?" Mary Gavin asked, nodding towards the ranch house.

"He's changing clothes." Haney said.

"What clothes?" Mary asked.

"The ones in his carpetbag, I reckon."

Suddenly Tom Janeen came out from the house wearing the tell-tale clothes of a gunman. His long sleeved shirt, vest, and pants were as black as night. So were his boots. The wide-brimmed, coal-black hat that had silver conchas across the brim. Around his waist he wore an oiled, beige-colored, leather belt, holster, and gun. The belt was full of bullets. Janeen carried another box in his hand.

Mary Gavin was amazed, almost thrilled, at the transformation from jailbird to gunslinger. This was the real Tom Janeen. She wondered how he would measure up against Farrell when they met.

Janeen put the extra bullets in the stallion's saddlebag, then went around to the front. He petted its forehead, whispering soothingly to it for several minutes. Finally the horse shook its head and nuzzled him. Janeen took the reins and climbed up in the saddle. Haney and Mary got on their mounts, too.

"Since we're heading west," Mary Gavin said, "we might as well stop at the line-shack. We should reach it by late afternoon. We can eat and bed down there."

"Good idea," Janeen said. "You lead, we'll follow."

Mary stared over at the ranch house for a moment and sighed, then nudged her horse. Haney and Janeen followed behind. She looked back again. Frank, Ray, and Ed were on the porch. She forced herself to wave. She hated good-byes.

They went out onto the road, but soon turned left into a grassy field. Here, the land was level, stretching to the west for miles. In three hours it began to slope down into a stand of silver aspen and birch to a well-worn trail. It eventually led into a vast area of low land that was full of light purple and yellow ground cover.

Two hours later they came upon a flat, treeless plain and saw cattle with the Lazy M brand on their flanks. Some were drinking from a wide, lazy stream that snaked in from the west then curled off to the east. They followed it for another two hours until it led them to the line-shack. By then it was almost sundown. The riders and the horses were ready to stop.

The line-shack had a larder with tins of hardtack, canned peaches, some salt-dried venison, and rabbit. It also had six bunks, a table, and four chairs. There were also tin plates with silverware. A small cast iron stove sat in one corner. Firewood was stacked against a wall.

They started a fire in the stove and Mary cooked up a meal. Sitting near the warmth of the stove, they talked.

"This is the end of my spread," Mary said. "From here on I'm lost, so you'll have to take the lead, Mr. Janeen."

Janeen nodded. "We'll head west towards Cheneyville. I figure we should be there by tomorrow afternoon. After that it's out into the badlands."

"We had best fill up as many canteens as we can, from the stream," Haney said. They all nodded.

By early evening of the next day the trio stopped at the cattle depot of Cheneyville to rest the horses. After they ate a hot meal at a beanery, Janeen sent a wire back to Marshal Leach in Brent's Ford. About twenty miles west of town they found a place to camp by a stream, built a fire and got their blanket rolls off their saddles. They hunkered down for the night.

The following morning they got up and headed into the Kansas badlands.

13.

They followed a rut-scarred road through a stretch of hardpan into a wooded area where it curved back and forth between the trees. Haney was in the lead when they saw seven scraggly masked men, with guns drawn, come out of the bushes and block the road. Haney, Janeen, and Mary stopped short.

"Get down, you ass holes or we'll blow you down!" the leader, who was in the center, said. He was wearing a ragged confederate army coat with sergeant's stripes and cap.

"I'll take the woman," one of the others chuckled. "You kin have the rest." They all looked like they needed a bath.

"No you don't, Fester! I saw her first!" a third one whined.

"Take it easy, now, friend," Haney said, dropping the reigns of his horse. He lowered his hands to his sides.

"I ain't asking you again, fool!" the leader yelled. "Get yer asses down!"

Janeen edged his horse up alongside Haney's.

"How much to let us pass, boss?" Janeen asked. "We'll be glad to pay."

"We'll take all you got, and the lady, too!" the leader growled.

"Sure, take it!" Janeen said calmly.

He drew his Colt and shot the leader between the eyes and dropped the two on the leader's left. As he was firing, Haney took out the two on the right. The remaining two ran off into the woods, firing wildly as they ran.

Art Haney took his hat off and looked at a bullet hole there. Janeen whistled. "That was close, kid."

"It was a lucky wild shot," Haney muttered.

"Let's go," Janeen said. They took off at a slow gallop. About three miles on the road they came out into open land and slowed down to a walk.

"The closer we get, the more of that we'll get" Janeen said. "So keep your eyes peeled."

For the rest of the day the land shifted from clusters of aspen, birch, and pine to scrub oak and hardpan. The road was worn smooth and it was an easy ride. They stopped in a small pine grove at noon to eat, drink, rest, and get out of the sun.

"How far?" Mary Gavin asked.

"I figure sometime tomorrow," Janeen said. "Sidewinder said it was about fifty miles west on the Cheneyville road."

"If he's harmed Sarah in any way, I want him to suffer," Mary said. "Promise me he'll suffer. I'll pay whatever you ask."

"He'll die like a rat, if he did," Haney said.

"It ain't going to be that easy," Janeen said. "He won't be alone."

"What's it like there?" Mary asked.

"Think of a scorpion's nest or a rattlesnake's den, that'll probably be about what it's like, ma'am."

Mary Gavin shivered. "That's not good, is it? What are our chances?"

"Not very good," Janeen said. "I'm hoping that Farrell's luck has run out and his stars aren't lined up."

Art Haney chuckled. "Well, that's encouraging."

"Things can turn on a dime, anytime and anyplace," Janeen said. "The thing is not to give up hope, even when it's hopeless."

"You were one of them once, weren't you?" Mary said to Janeen.

He nodded. "I was, yes. And that makes it all the worse."

"Why?" Mary asked.

Haney cut in, "They know he got amnesty, went to prison, and got a pardon. He broke the code and to them he's as bad as any lawman."

"Oh, dear," Mary muttered. "This doesn't look good."

In half an hour they were back on the road. The sky started to cloud over and it began to rain. Ten minutes after that, they were soaked. It was refreshing and cool. By dark, they pulled off the road into a stand of birch trees. The rain turned colder so they sat with their backs together to keep warm. The one thing they had left behind were their rain slickers.

Sometime after midnight the rain slacked off and it turned even colder. It cleared up and the moon came out.

They could hear coyotes howling off in the distance. Once a wild dog came up and sniffed them. When Mary Gavin reached out to pet it, it ran off as if stung.

"Sarah always wanted a dog," she said. "If we get her out of this, I'll get her one. A German shepherd."

"Those are good dogs," Haney said. "They'll die to protect you."

"Yes, good dogs," Mary said. She nodded slowly. Soon she was asleep.

In a few minutes Art Haney was asleep, too. Tom Janeen stayed awake, listening and looking, aware of everything around him, clutching his gun in his hand. He was still alert when the other two woke up to a clear bright sky. He had sat up all night, on guard.

They made breakfast and were on the road again within two hours.

The road lay straight ahead for about a mile, then went up and disappeared behind a slope. They walked their horses at a casual, energy-saving pace, keeping a look out for ruts and holes. A horse with a broken leg would be a disaster.

Finally they reached the top of the rise and stopped to look down.

There, below them, in the middle of a bare, open area, was a single structure. It was broad and squat, and had earthen, berm-mound walls and a sod roof. In front was a door with a piece of soiled canvas over it. Smoke rose from a stove-pipe chimney that stuck up in the back. A dozen horses were tied to the rail in front.

They had reached the Devil's Den, at last.

14.

Sunk halfway into the ground, and with a flat, sod roof, the Devil's Den stood as a sanctuary in the desolation of the Kansas badlands. It was the last oasis for the bottom-feeders, social outcasts, and fugitives from justice that roamed the outskirts of western civilization. Murderers, swindlers, bank and train robbers, and anyone dodging the long arm of the law, knew that the Devil's Den was their safe haven. If a lawman went there, he never left alive.

Art Haney, Tom Janeen, and Mary Gavin approached the Devil's Den at a slow, wary pace. They stopped and stood staring at the door, listening to the steady roar of voices that came out through the canvas covered threshold. Janeen was the first to dismount and tie his horse to the rail. Haney and Mary did the same.

Janeen and Haney checked their guns. The older man went in first. Haney and Mary followed. It was like going down into the bowels of hell.

A dense shroud of suffocating smoke from oil lamps, hand rolled cigarettes, and cigars billowed about on undulating currents. The hard-packed earthen floor was covered with soiled sawdust, gravel, and broken glass from beer and whiskey bottles. A dozen circular tables were scattered about where jackals, snakes, and other misfits of humanity drank, smoked, chewed, spit, and passed wind over games of cards and dice.

The three intruders stood adjusting their eyes. The smell was so bad Mary Gavin had to cover her nose and mouth with her hand. Eventually Janeen spotted the bar and they squeezed past a labyrinth of tables to get to it.

Suddenly the room seemed to grow quiet. The bartender, a huge, bull of a man, came out of the shadows. He laid his massive paws on the bar and glared at Mary Gavin.

"You ain't allowed in here, lady. You better leave pronto!"

"We're looking for Rice Farrell. Is he here?" Janeen said.

A voice in the dark, behind them, yelled out, "Hey, fellows, look, it's Kid Janeen!"

Another said, "Naw, he's up in the state pen with old Sidewinder! It can't be Kid Janeen."

Suddenly four scrawny gunmen came out of somewhere. They made a place for themselves at the bar.

"You a friend of Farrell's," one of them asked.

"I've got something for him," Janeen said.

"You do, huh?"

"Yep."

"Well, give it to me and I'll see he gets it."

"I'm saving it especially for him," Janeen said.

The gunman stepped back and turned to the tables. "Hey! I think we got a bounty hunter here, fellahs!"

Suddenly a dozen dirt-caked, scab-infested outcasts rose from the tables and converged on the bar.

"I don't want no trouble, men! They was just leaving," the bartender whined.

He started to reach under the bar for his scattergun but stopped when a half dozen gun barrels were shoved in his face. He raised his hands and backed away.

Suddenly a voice came from somewhere in the shadows.

"Somebody looking for me?" Rice Farrell came strutting up to the bar. "Well, well, if it isn't the widow Gavin. What brings you to this neck of the woods, ma'am?"

Mary Gavin faced Farrell, staring into his eyes. "Mr. Farrell, please give me my little girl. I'm begging. Please, sir."

Farrell chuckled. "I liked you better when you were a cold as ice bitch, Mrs. Gavin." He turned to Haney and Janeen. "Well looky here, Tom Janeen and Art Haney! This is my lucky day!"

"Come outside and we'll see how lucky you are, you son-of-a-bitch!" Haney said menacingly.

Farrell smiled and looked over at Tom Janeen. "I've been hoping I'd meet up with you again, Janeen. You once told me you were the fastest draw in the west, remember?"

Suddenly Janeen yelled, "Hey, fellahs! Rice Farrell here is a cradle snatcher! He's kidnapped this woman's little girl. He's broken the code!"

There was an eerie silence. Farrell looked uncertain for a moment. Suddenly he turned and yelled, "This is Kid Janeen, boys! He got amnesty while Sidewinder still sits in prison! Whatta we do with squealers, men?"

"We hang 'em," someone in the back hollered.

"Cut his balls off," another screamed.

Farrell slapped Janeen hard across the face. Janeen flinched and shook the slap off, rubbing his cheek.

"That'll cost you one belly button, Farrell," Janeen said.

For a moment Farrell wondered what that meant. He chuckled and turned to the men at the bar.

"Put their gun hands on the bar, boys," Farrell said.

Haney and Janeen went for their guns but never made it. Grabbed by half a dozen outlaws, they were pinned facedown against the bar with their gun hands laid out flat. Farrell asked for a pistol. He took it and, using it as a hammer, he smashed the knuckles of both their hands. The two men gasped in pain. Mary Gavin moaned and leaned against the bar for support.

Farrell gave the man back his pistol. "Take these two dumb-asses outside," he growled. Two big men grabbed Haney and Janeen and dragged them out through the doorway. Farrell turned his full attention to Mary Gavin.

"You want to play stuck up with me, now, Mrs. Gavin?" Farrell smirked.

"Please. Sir. My little girl!"

Farrell chuckled. "She's a big girl now."

Mary Gavin groaned and lashed out, raking her fingernails down Farrell's left forehead and cheek, close to his eye, leaving three bloody furrows. Farrell winced in pain and grunted. He stepped back and stared at Mary Gavin.

"I killed your husband!" Farrell hissed sadistically and slammed his fist into Mary Gavin's face, knocking her to her knees. She groaned in pain and shook her head to keep from fainting. Blood ran from her nose. She stayed down, slumped against the bar.

"I'll be back in a minute, Mrs. Gavin," Farrell said. "Then, we'll have a party." He went outside.

When Farrell's men saw him, they spread out, leaving a space between him and the two intruders, laughing and chatting among themselves. Rice Farrell was going to put on a show. It would end with Haney and Janeen lying dead on the ground with a slug in their hearts. These outlaws had seen this play many times before.

115

Haney and Janeen had managed to wrap their injured gun hands in their bandannas. Using their good hands, they had tucked their guns into the waistbands of their trousers with the handles pointing to the left. Haney looked at Janeen.

"What's Farrell up to?"

"Nothing much," Janeen said. "He's just gonna kill us, that's about all."

"Oh," Haney said, "for a minute I was worried."

Janeen looked around. "This dance ain't over yet, kid."

"You got a plan?" Haney asked.

"I'm thinking."

"Well, hurry it up, will ya?"

Finally Janeen said. "You do what you gotta do, but I'm gonna do a belly whopper."

"A lot of good that'll do ya," Haney chuckled.

They turned to look down the empty space to where Farrell was wiping blood off his left forehead and cheek.

"Looks like Mrs. Gavin got a good lick in," Janeen said.

"Yeah and this just might be the edge we need," Haney replied.

He and Janeen could see Farrell was having trouble stopping the blood on his forehead from blurring the vision in his left eye. He finally got it under control and stopped dabbing at it with his bandanna.

"You okay, Rice old buddy?" someone shouted.

"I'm fine, my man!" Farrell shouted. The crowd roared.

The onlookers watched as Farrell did some fancy gun twirling and flipping to limber up, flexing his fingers together and cracking his knuckles. He tossed his gun high, making it cartwheel, and catching it behind his back as it came down. The crowd yelled and applauded. Someone shouted his name, and soon they were chanting it again and again. Farrell let it go on for a while, basking in the adulation. Finally it faded away. They now wanted action.

Farrell stared down the open area at Haney and Janeen.

"You who are about to die, do you have any last words?" he shouted.

"Can I step back a mile or two, I'm farsighted," Haney said. A few in the crowd laughed.

Janeen looked at Haney. "I don't know about you, but I'm going for the belly button, just like I told him."

"I might just try the right eye," Haney said.

"If you make it, I'll give you a double-eagle," Janeen said.

"I'll hold you to that Kid Janeen," Haney said with a chuckle.

"They used to call me that when I was about your age, Haney. But I grew up."

"Oh!" Haney chuckled.

Suddenly Rice Farrell took up the gun fighter's stance, and glared across the space between them. His finger's danced with nervous anticipation. One leg twitched.

"Draw!" Farrell screamed suddenly, as loud as he could.

Art Haney started quickly backing up as he drew. He fired one shot. Tom Janeen leaped to the right, firing once in mid-air. He landed with a grunt on his belly, in the dirt, his eye still on the target.

Rice Farrell had a confused look on his face. He coughed once, looked around, smiled, and slowly sat down in the dirt, soiling his pants. He died never realizing he had been shot both in his right eye, and in his belly button.

Janeen got up quickly. He and Haney trained their guns on the crowd.

"Scatter!" Haney yelled.

In a moment's flicker, there was a mad dash for the horses and the outcasts left in a cloud of dust, pounding away into the distance. Janeen and Haney looked at each other and shrugged.

"Pretty good, kid," Janeen said. "You have the voice of authority." He chuckled and winced in pain, favoring his injured hand.

They went down inside the Devil's Den. Two men were holding Mary Gavin up by the arms to keep her from falling. One had his gun to her head. Her nose dripped blood.

"Farrell is dead," Janeen yelled from the doorway.

"Yeah? Well, we ain't." one of them yelled back.

"You will be," Haney said loudly.

"You two ride out, and we'll have some fun with this bitch," the one with the gun said.

"I don't have time for this," Haney muttered. He drew with his good hand and fanned his Colt, dropping both of the gunmen with two shots. Tom Janeen rushed up to catch Mary Gavin. She collapsed in is arms.

Suddenly the bartender and his wife came out from the back. Sarah Gavin was with them. She rushed up to her mother and hugged and kissed her.

"The girl's okay. I looked after her," the old lady said.

"Thank you, ma'am,' Art Haney said.

He reached into his pocket and took out several gold double-eagles and placed them on the bar. He went to Sarah who was sobbing over her mother. "We'd better get going."

Mary Gavin held onto the bar. "I don't feel very well, Mr. Janeen. Would you please help me?"

Tom Janeen picked her up in his arms and they went outside. "I'm getting you all bloody, Mr. Janeen," Mary said weakly. "I'm so sorry."

"It's okay, Mary."

"Mrs. Gavin, sir."

Janeen chuckled. "Mrs. Gavin, ma'am."

While Mary Gavin leaned against the packhorse, Tom Janeen got a cloth from the supply bag. He wet it from a canteen and gave it to Sarah to wipe the blood off her mother's face. He waited until Mary Gavin was settled then lifted her up to put her on the big stallion's saddle. He tied her horse behind the packhorse. He got up behind her and nudged the big horse into a gentle walk. Sarah and Art Haney followed in the same fashion.

The four of them went down the road towards Cheneyville. By the time they got to the stand of birch trees the sun was down. Janeen spread out blankets for the women while Haney made a small fire. They ate some beef jerky then had some hardtack and coffee.

Hours later, when Sarah and Haney were asleep, Mary Gavin went to Tom Janeen and kissed him on the mouth and thanked him.

"Does that mean I can call you Mary?" Janeen chuckled.

"Not yet," she said. "Maybe later."

15.

They arose early in the morning and moved on again. Mary Gavin was in pain so Janeen went along cautiously to avoid bumps and jolts. They reached Cheneyville by dark, stayed overnight in a hotel, and started out again in the morning.

Three days later they reached the Lazy M line-shack. It was late afternoon so they stayed there to eat and rest for the night. When they finished, Mary took Sarah aside and spoke to her.

"Did Farrell touch you, Sarah?"

"No, mother."

"You needn't lie, baby. It's best to tell."

"He didn't, momma. He said…"

"He said what?"

"He said he was gonna take me to Utah. We were going to join the Mormons there, and get married, and I'd be his wife. He said his mother and father were Mormons. I think he was a little bit crazy, momma."

Mary Gavin let out a big sigh of relief. She shook her head. "Yes, baby, he was crazy. Crazy as a loon." She slept better that night.

The next day they rose at sunrise to get an early start, and by noontime they rode wearily into the yard of the Lazy M. As they dismounted, Ed, Frank, and Ray ran out to greet them.

"Momma! What happened to your nose," little Ray shouted. "Did you fall off your horse?"

"You guys look awful!" Ed said.

"Oh, shut up, Ed Gavin," Sarah said. "You weren't any help!" She went into the house in a huff.

"Ed," Mary Gavin said, "you and Frank take care of the horses. They'll need oats and water, and a good rub down."

Frank and Ed grabbed the horse's reins and led them over to what was left of the barn.

Suddenly, as they stood there, they heard a noise. They looked. A cloud of dust was rising down the road, moving in their direction. Mary Gavin shaded her eyes, staring. The cloud continued to get bigger. Pretty soon she could see a lot of people on buckboards and wagons headed in the direction of the Lazy M. Six wagons pulled into the yard. Four were full of lumber and two were full of people from the adjoining ranches and towns. Mary knew most of them. They waved and yelled to her.

Their leader, Amory Stone, came up to her.

"How do, Mary," Stone said.

"Amory, glad to see you."

"What happened to your nose, Mary? Or shouldn't I ask?"

"Better not to ask, Amory," Mary said.

"I understand," Amory replied. "We'll have your bunkhouse and barn up in about a week. Then we'll have us a big barn dance. How does that sound?"

"Amory, I could kiss you right here and now."

"Best not, my wife might get the wrong idea, Mary," Amory said, blushing. He turned and walked off to join the others.

Suddenly the Marshal came riding up. When he saw Mary Gavin he dismounted and rushed over to her, removing his hat.

"My God, Mary! What did you do?"

"We went and got my daughter back, Marshal," Mary said. "And don't ask me what happened to my nose, please."

"Alright, I won't. Is Sarah okay?"

"Under the circumstances, yes, thanks to Mr. Haney and Mr. Janeen and, strangely enough, to Mr. Farrell. But I'll tell you all about that, later."

The Marshal looked at the two men, noticing their injured hands. "How did that happen?"

"A souvenir from Farrell's men," Haney said. "But Janeen and I left them with a few souvenirs of our own."

"Farrell, is he dead?"

"Sort of," Janeen said.

The Marshal looked at Janeen. "You're in parole violation. You know that, don't you?"

"What? The clothes or the gun?"

"Both," the Marshal said.

125

"Yeah, I suppose I am," Janeen said.

Mary Gavin gave the Marshal a stern look.

"However, if you was to go into that house and come out dressed like you was a week ago, I could offer you amnesty, like the…"

"The railroad?" Janeen asked.

"Yeah, just like the railroad," the Marshal said.

"I'll take you up on that offer, Marshal!"

Tom Janeen went into the house. Art Haney followed him. The Marshal looked at Mary Gavin. "Maybe I shouldn't say this, Mary, but you should have someone."

"Are you proposing, Marshal?"

The Marshal chuckled. "Heavens, no, Mary, not that I, well, you know what I mean."

"Are you referring to Mr. Janeen, Marshal?"

"I suppose I am, Mary."

"I've only been a widow for a short while, you know."

"That's true, Mary, but this is not like back east. Life out here plays hard and fast. You have to take what you can when you can get it or you might live the rest of your life regretting having passed up a chance for happiness."

"That's quite a speech, Marshal," Mary said. "I didn't know you were such a romantic person."

The Marshal almost blushed. "Me? Romantic? Gosh, no!"

Tom Janeen came out of the ranch house dressed in his blue prison suit. Mary laughed. "I'll have to take you into town to Price's Mercantile for some decent clothes, Mr. Janeen."

Janeen chuckled. "Yeah, I guess I do look funny, don't I?

"Yes," Mary said. "You look like a salesman. Especially when you carry that carpetbag around."

The Marshal chuckled.

Janeen turned to the Marshal. "What's with Dagston? Is he still around?"

"No, not anymore, I took your advice and wired the Pinkertons, in Chicago. The very next day they sent in three detectives on the train. Dagston spotted them and tried to

127

make a run for it. He didn't get very far. He's gone now. Bank embezzlement, he's facing thirty years."

I ran over his foot," Mary said. "With the buckboard wheel."

"Yeah," the Marshal said "He was in pain when they took him away. Kind of sad, though, when you think about it. He gave me this job. I liked him. He did a lot for the town."

"Yes, that's true. He had a gift for business," Mary said. "He did a lot for the people. Everyone liked him. He helped build the church and brought in a doctor. But he got too greedy, I guess."

"What about Charley, the bartender?" Janeen asked. "Is he still around?"

"I forgot to tell you. He and his men were in on that fight for the Lazy M. They found his body in front of the bunkhouse. What's left of his men have gone off to God knows where, looking for work, I suppose."

"Very sad," Mary Gavin said.

"Yes, Charley seemed like a nice fellah," Janeen said.

"Janeen," the Marshal said, "why don't you take Mrs. Gavin into the house? I think she's ready to sit down to a hot cup of coffee."

"I'm fine, Marshal," Mary said.

"No you're not," Janeen said. He swept Mary up in his arms, and started carrying her towards the ranch house porch.

"I'm only following the Marshal's orders, ma'am," Janeen said.

"Tom Janeen," Mary said. "After all we've been through together, why aren't you calling me Mary?"

"But I thought…"

"Never mind what you thought, Tom Janeen."

"But…"

"No, 'but's'. If you don't call me Mary, I shall be very angry."

"But…"

"Oh, hush!"

"Can I take you to that barn dance next week, Mrs. Gavin? I mean, Mary."

"Of course you can, you silly man."

Tom Janeen carried his bride-to-be over the threshold, into the ranch house. They could hear their neighbors beginning work on the new barn, chattering and laughing. Some even hummed and sang. They worked fast and hard, knowing that one of their own was in need of help. It was their way, the way of the west: Always come to the aid of a neighbor.

The End.

About the Author

R. Annan is a seasoned and traveled author with many interests. As a career serviceman he served in Korea and Vietnam. He also completed a one-year course at the Defense Language Institute at Monterey, California, and graduated from the University of South Florida with a B.A. in Art and Art History. After taking a two-year course in screenwriting at the Hollywood Scriptwriting Institute, he established *The Old Time Radio Club Time Machine* as both a scriptwriter and an actor.

A Note from the Author

Thank you for reading my book. If you enjoyed it, would you please consider rating and reviewing it? I'd enjoy your feedback. Thank you!